A SPECIAL PLACE

A SPECIAL PLACE

The Heart of a Dark Matter

——

PETER STRAUB

PEGASUS BOOKS
New York

A SPECIAL PLACE

Pegasus Books LLC
80 Broad Street, 5th Floor
New York, NY 10004

ISBN: 978-1-60598-102-4

10 9 8 7 8 6 5 4 3 2 1

Printed in the United States of America
Distributed by W. W. Norton & Company, Inc.

A SPECIAL PLACE

MILWAUKEE, 1958

"YOU'RE GOING TO NEED A SPECIAL PLACE ONLY YOU know about," Uncle Till told Keith Hayward. They were seated on a broad tree stump in the backyard of the Hayward family home, where Uncle Till was a temporary guest. Keith was twelve years old. This conversation took place in mid-July, high summer, 1958, when Milwaukee was hot and humid from morning to midnight. Tillman Hayward's thin,

3

sleeveless T-shirt clung to the sides of his chest and exposed his muscular arms and shoulders. The tilted brim of his gray fedora shaded most of his handsome, long-nosed face, though sweat shone on his cheeks and pooled in the dark hollows at the base of his throat. Tucked in at the knee, his blue pinstriped trousers floated their cuffs nearly a foot above his shiny black wingtips. The coolest suspenders Keith had ever seen, of braided leather no thicker than a pencil, held up the unpleated waistband of the trousers. This man, Tillman Hayward, knew how to dress.

"And let's say you get a place like that, because I'm just saying like, what if? *If* you get a special place all your own, you should be able to lock it up, so no one else can get in. What goes on in that room is private. Nobody should know about it but you. See, if let's say you happen to go down this path, you're gonna have all kinds of secrets."

"Like this is secret, what we're talking about," Keith said.

"Bull's-eye! Home run! You got it! Let's go through it again. Your daddy or your pretty momma ask what we were talking about after I warned you about those experiments, the answer is. . . . ?"

"Baseball." Keith had been thoroughly prepped on this point.

"*Baseball*," Till agreed. "That's right. Warren Spahn, greatest pitcher in the National League. Del Crandall, greatest catcher in the National League. Eddie Matthews, greatest *guy* in the National League, right?"

"Right."

"Now *you* tell me their names, boy."

"Warren Spahn, Spahnie. Del Crandall, the catcher. Eddie Mathews, third base. They're the greatest."

In truth, Keith cared nothing for baseball. He didn't see the point of all that throwing and hitting and running when nothing was at stake but the outcome of a stupid game. Everyone around him, including the other kids at school, his parents, and even the teachers and the principal, pretty much everybody in the world except Uncle Till, acted like Jesus himself would stand up if one of the Milwaukee Braves walked into the room.

"Attaway. So anyhow, let's say we got this special

place, this secret room. You know what you need to keep it secret? I already gave you a big hint."

"A key to lock it up." Hoping he had understood his uncle's point about *what if*, Keith took a big step into the dark. "That's if, you know, I happened to have a place like that."

"Oh, you're something," said Uncle Till. "Yes, you are."

Keith's face blazed with pleasure; satisfaction glowed in his stomach with the warmth of a good meal.

"Again, just supposing here, just saying *what if*, if you should happen to get the key you need, I could give you a great idea about that. This key we're talking about shouldn't have to sit out in the world all naked and exposed, where anyone might come along and ask questions about it. I mean, what kind of secret would that be?"

"No good, that's what it would be," said Keith, feeling a kind of anticipatory shame wavering flamelike inside of him.

"Damn straight, boy. Now, nothing hides a little key better than a bunch of other keys. We're still playing the *what if* game here, so I'd say if a fellow was interested in the kind of stuff we're talking about, for one reason or another, one smart thing he could do would be to pick up every stray key he happens to find and string them on a good key ring. You come across old keys lyin' around all over the place, once you start looking for them. In drawers. On desks. In any old place, and by the way, some old building nobody goes into any more, oh, an abandoned house, an empty old warehouse, anything like that, would be a good place to find your secret room. And the basement generally works out real good. God bless basements, is my motto."

The boy had a sudden thought, a vision more than a thought, of an abandoned building located six or seven blocks distant on their nearby commercial avenue. Once it had housed a diner, later on a bar, and after that it had been the place of worship for some religious cult so marginal that the neighbors had actually driven them off in a spasm of high-mindedness. "Like that old dump on Sherman Boulevard?"

"Is there an old dump on Sherman Boulevard?" Uncle Till's eyes shone. "Imagine that."

"I *thi-i-i-i-nk* so," Keith said, really getting into the game.

"Might be worth a closer look, I don't know. To a fellow interested in that kind of thing, anyhow."

Keith nodded, trying to picture the building in more detail. For a while, the neighborhood teenagers had prowled through its empty rooms, leaving behind dirty mattresses, cigarette butts, beer bottles, and limp condoms, but he had the feeling that it had been left alone for a long time now. The building had a basement, of that he was almost certain.

"I could give you a little tip," his uncle said, capturing his attention once again. "Let's say a person puts together a nice big key ring, fifty keys, a hundred, how does he manage to put his hand on the one or two he actually needs? Well, this is how. You take a little bit of string and tie it in a knot right next to the important keys, and then you can find them in a jif."

From what must have been the extraordinarily deep pocket of the elegant trousers he produced a giant ball of keys and rattled it before his nephew's eyes. Here and there, tiny bits of colored string protruded from it.

"When a man carries a ball of keys like this, nobody ever asks him what he's doing. As good as a badge."

The screen door banged. With a slow, uncertain step, Keith's mother emerged onto the back steps. Her anxious gaze took them both in. At the ends of her rigid arms, her hands hung like tight knots.

"Have a good talk?" The contrast between her question and her demeanor struck Keith as humorous. He nodded, trying not to smile.

"Till?"

"It's fine, Mags," said Uncle Till. "There's nothing to worry about. We have here a fine, fine boy. That poor cat was dead when he found it. No reason to bother Bill about all this. The boy and I have had a good talk. Haven't we, kiddo?"

Nodding, Keith said, "We sure have."

In Maggie Hayward's regard could be read the degree to which she wanted to believe everything her brother-in-law had told her, as well as all that he had implied. "But what about the knife? What about the cat's head?"

"Guilty as charged. I think we can put that down to Keith's sense of curiosity."

"I wanted to see how it was connected," Keith said. "You know, the bones and stuff."

"Scientific impulse, pure and simple," said Uncle Till. "I explained that Keith really has to wait for high school biology before he starts to dissect things. Including any dead animals he might come across in that old vacant lot."

At the beginning of the most rewarding conversation of Keith's entire life, Uncle Till had in fact said something very like this.

"I know better now, Mom," Keith said.

Keith's mother began to move down the three concrete steps to ground level. Her elbows struck a slight angle, and her hands were unclenched. When she hit the bottom step, anguish and disgust momentarily contorted her face. "Well, I hope so, because I just hated seeing . . . It made me feel so *awful* . . ."

"Of course it did, honey." Uncle Till stood up and

slipped the ball of keys back into his capacious pocket. "I'd feel the same way myself."

"Sorry, Mom," Keith said. "I'll never do it again."

"I hope *not*." She gave them both a tentative smile. "I'm glad you were here to talk to Keith, Till. And you're right, I don't want to bother Bill with all this stuff. It's over and done with, right?"

"Right," Keith said.

"It looked like you were showing him your keys," she said.

"That I was, Mags, that I was. Here's my thinking. My nephew needs a hobby, that's pretty clear. So I was recommending he go around collecting keys, the way I do. You can get a lot of pleasure out of an old key, imagining all the people that used it and what kind of door it opened."

"Do you like that idea?" his mother asked. She seemed skeptical, with some reason.

"Yeah," he said. "I really do."

"It'd be good for you to have a hobby. Maybe I can keep my eye out for old keys, help you start your collection."

"That would be great, Mom."

Keith glanced up at his uncle. The shadow of his hat brim made a jutting slab of his nose, as though his were one of the faces on Mount Rushmore.

"This boy is going to do just fine," Till said. "Yep, he's on his way. Now let's put the cherry on top. I wouldn't be surprised if one day, Keith turned out to be a doctor. That's right. An honest-to-God, actual M.D. Rise and shine, pretty lady. Your boy has all the tools he'll ever need. He just has to figure out how to put his hands on 'em."

Beneath everything his uncle said, Keith thought, ran another line of thought altogether, intended only for him.

———

Although he lived in Columbus, Ohio, Tillman Hayward had been staying in his brother Bill's house for a couple of weeks. This information was a secret to all but the family. He slept on the old family bed in the spare room, and now and again he joined the others for meals. Till sometimes stuck around in the evenings to make cutting remarks about *Gunsmoke*, or *The Rifleman,* or whatever they had gathered to watch on the TV, but usually he snuck out in his snappy clothes around nine or ten at night and did not return until just before dawn. Uncle Till did not have an ordinary job. He did "deals" and made "arrangements," he "put things together." Bill Hayward, Keith's father, was putting in his twelfth year on the spray line at Continental Can, and he envied his brother's freedom. Ever since his foreman's application had been denied, Bill came home grudging and morose, grumbling about his job and reeking of solvent. To his younger brother, Tillman's good luck and handsome face had allowed him to escape the prison of blue-collar life. The man was a kind of magician, and whatever he did to remain afloat could not be judged by the usual systems.

Above them both hovered the example of their oldest and best-looking sibling, Margaret Frances, who had changed her name to Margot, talked her way into a good job at a radio station in Minneapolis, and married a poleaxed millionaire named Rudy. Margaret Frances/Margot had never been much for family anyhow, and after the birth of her first child,

Mortimer, she stopped even sending out Christmas cards. Margaret Frances/Margot had struck it rich, and who could say that Tillman, almost as attractive, would not do the same?

Uncle Till enjoyed a series called *Peter Gunn*. He thought he looked a lot like Craig Stevens, the dark-haired actor playing a private detective who wore expensive suits and hung out in a jazz club. Keith could see the resemblance, though he thought his uncle often operated on the other side of the law from Peter Gunn. Presumably this trait lay behind the secrecy about his uncle's presence in their house. His parents maintained a steadfast vagueness on the issue. Bill Hayward explained the necessity to inform women that Tilly was elsewhere by referring to the sheer number of dames who wanted to get their mitts on him. Hell, the guy *had* to hide out! This obligation to deny Tillman's presence in their house extended to men as well. Instead of calling, the men tended to come over and ring the bell. You couldn't just wait for them to go away, because these guys had no manners. They pushed the buzzer and pounded the door, sometimes yelling, until someone came out to talk to them. They called themselves friends, but they were bill collectors; they said they wanted to pay back a loan, but they were really pissed-off husbands. Or they were cops looking to close old cases by pinning them on Tillman Hayward, whom they secretly envied.

"They should, too," Keith's father said. "Till's got radar they only dream about. My brother, he knows things. He can tell when a cop is keeping an eye on the house, so he just holes up in his room until they go away. Fact is, he'd of been a better cop than any of those clowns on the city payroll. Only, he never wanted to be just a hard-ass with a gun."

A couple of days each week, Uncle Till squirreled himself away in the old spare room at the back of the house, curled up in blankets and read the paper, listening to the radio, drinking bourbon, sometimes propping his back against the headboard and wrapping his arms around his knees while he stared at the colorless walls. The man always wore his hat, even in bed. Keith thought that was amazingly cool.

"Keith, get out of there and leave your uncle alone," his mother yelled. "Till doesn't want a little boy hanging on to him every second of the day."

"I don't mind the kid," Uncle Till yelled back. "Fact is, he's good company."

There were days Till's radar told him he could not even walk out through the kitchen door into the back garden. They were watching the house that closely – some days, he had to be careful not to walk past the windows.

"I didn't do any of the stuff they want to pin on me," he said. "I'm not saying I never crossed the line, because that's what the line is for. But the Chief of Police here, Brier, is a showboat. He thinks cops ought to be able to shoot *jaywalkers*. Brier would love to put my ass in jail."

He looked down at his nephew, and his face darkened. "You know what's going to happen? One day some cop is going to jump out of an alley right in front of you. This cop is going to ask you, do you know where we can find your uncle Till? Is he staying at your house, Keith? We just want to talk to him, can't you give us a hand? And you say . . ."

"I don't know where he is. But I wish he'd come back, because we used to talk about baseball."

"What a kid this is," he said, and leaned forward to rumple Keith's hair. "You and me, right? You and me."

"You and me," Keith repeated, glowing within.

Another time, Keith peeked around his uncle's door, found him sitting up in bed with his hat on his head, staring at nothing, looking inside himself, the boy thought. Till came out of his trance, invited him in, and wound up telling him about his favorite movies.

"There's this man, one day you're gonna love him as much as I do. Alfred Hitchcock, the master of suspense, they call him. Could be the greatest movie director of all time. Ever hear of the guy?"

"Maybe," Keith said, hoping that his uncle would just go on and on, and not stop to ask him questions. The long muscles under his skin, the angles of his face, the beauty of the hat brim, the poise of his hands, and the curl of smoke rising from the cigarette tilted between his fingers: all of this, and more, he wanted to take in and memorize.

"For my money, his greatest movie is that new one, *Vertigo*. Came out this year. *Crazy*, crazy movie, kiddo. These blondes, they're all the same woman but you don't know that, they're always falling out of windows and off cliffs, and you *know* the bitches won't survive, hell, pardon my French, you know these *women* are either gonna hit the ground or slam against the water and go under, so if they don't drown they're gonna get squashed like a bug. Tightened my throat, Keith. And this guy, Jimmy Stewart, only the *bad* Jimmy Stewart, like his crazy twin, he follows the blonde into this art museum and he stares at her staring at a painting, and he keeps on staring and she keeps on staring, it's so *weird*, there's no one else in this big old room but them, and finally you have to stare at the painting, too. It's really terrible, it's like a damn cartoon! Hell, you say to yourself, this painting's a fake! You'd never find crap like that in a fancy museum. So then you realize half the backgrounds in the movie are complete fakes, too, and the girl is also a complete fake, and the hero is out of his mind, and besides, he's cruel as shit, you should see the way he treats that girl . . ."

Uncle Till smiled. For a moment, he looked like a cat with a moth trapped beneath its paws.

"Could be the greatest movie of all time. Damn near made me see double. Soon as I got out, I had to go to a bar. *But.* And this is a big, big but. Hitchcock's *second*-greatest movie could have been even better. Slides along like shit on silk. *Shadow of a Doubt.* Came out in I think 1943. You ever see that movie?"

"I don't think so."

"Nah, you weren't even born then, were you? You have to see *Shadow of a Doubt,* though. The great Joseph Cotten, man, if it weren't for Lawrence Tierney and Richard Widmark, he'd be my favorite actor. Only problem with that movie is, Hitchcock loused up the ending. The creeps that own the studios, man, they must have seen what was going on in this movie and sent him a message, pronto. There was a knock on the door, and when he opened it, a big ol' knee-breaker hands him a piece of paper that says, *Change the ending of your movie, or we're gonna burn down your house and kill your wife.* They had to step in and screw things up."

"Why?"

"They want things to look a certain way, see? Right is right, and wrong is wrong, and that's the whole deal. If what they call 'right' doesn't win every time, the suckers in the balcony are gonna get pissed off.

"So what happens in *Shadow of a Doubt?* Joseph Cotten, Uncle Charlie, arrives in the California town where his sister is married to this dodo. They have a good-looking teenage daughter. The sister and the niece love Joseph Cotten, he's the apple of their eye. The whole first half of the movie is like that. Only, us guys sitting out there stuffing our faces with popcorn gradually get the idea that good old Joseph Cotten has a whopper of a dark side, and it has to do with women.

"I mean, that's okay, isn't it? It *ought* to be, for anybody who lives in the real world. If they made a movie about you and me, would you want me to get killed at the end?"

Keith shook his head.

"That's why I know the creeps at the studio made Alfred Hitchcock kill off Uncle Charlie at the end of the movie instead of doing it right. Because the *real* ending would have had Uncle Charlie and the girl going away together as what you could call partners in crime."

"Crime," Keith said, growing even more interested. A ball made of burning nettles was squeezing upward within his throat, and he swallowed to keep it down. "What kind of crime?"

Uncle Till motioned him forward. He face darkened and glittered as the boy approached. When Keith had come close enough, he extended his elegant left arm, gripped his nephew's shoulder with his powerful fingers, and pulled him down until the boy's ear was close to his mouth. He smelled of musky aftershave, tobacco, and dried sweat.

"In the real world?"

He chuckled, and Keith's giblets thrilled.

"Here's what they'd do. They'd get women to give them their money, and then they'd kill them. I don't know how they'd do it, but for sure, if it was *me*, I'd use a knife."

His uncle relaxed his grip. Face burning, Keith straightened up. If he'd had a year to think about it, he still could not have described the tumult going on within him. Uncle Till, utterly relaxed, smiled back from the deep, hidden center of his being. A godlike amusement seemed to irradiate his features as he raised his chin and leveled his eyes at a point only he could see. "Know what the newspapers in *Shadow of a Doubt* were calling good old Uncle Charlie? The Honeymoon Killer. It's funny, how they can libel you with a handle like that."

"Yeah," Keith said, uncertain of the point.

"It's exactly like some reporter in the *Milwaukee Journal* wrote this story where he called you the Pussycat Killer. The Tabby Killer. That wouldn't seem right, would it?"

The flush on the boy's face turned a deeper red. "No."

"There's so much more *to* it. You know what I'm talking about."

Maggie Hayward's voice floated in from the kitchen, telling Keith to give his uncle some peace. This time, Till waved him away.

He walked down the hallway toward the kitchen. A tangle of thoughts and emotions rolled from his chest to his head and back again. He felt as though Uncle Till had sunk a branding iron into his brain. *You know what I'm talking about.*

Did he?

If it was me, I'd use a knife.

Was his uncle talking about actually using a knife? How using a knife made you feel? He could never have described how he had felt when, after a titanic battle, he had at last cornered the spitting, hissing cat in the vacant lot at the end of their block and rammed the carving knife into its belly.

He entered the kitchen hoping to pass unnoticed. His mother turned from her cooking and gave his face the customary inspection. From the big metal pot simmering on the stove came a thick odor of carrots, onions, and softening beef. Whatever Maggie Hayward saw in his face made her lower her eyebrows and peer at him more closely. For an uncomfortable moment, her eyes sought and found his own. The moment of live contact underscored the new recognition that Keith and his mother lately had become almost exactly the same height, a fact that both unsettled and excited him.

A ladle slick with pale brown fluid drooped from her right hand.

"Keith, your face is bright red," she told him. "Do you have a fever?"

"I don't think so."

She came closer and pressed her free hand to his forehead. Keith watched stuff like gravy begin to drip onto the patterned blue linoleum.

"Mom," he said. "Your spoon, um."

"Oh, drat," she said, and in a single movement spun sideways to drop the ladle beside the sink, grab a paper towel, bend down, and wipe away the tiny stain. The paper towel flew into the garbage pail.

"What do you and Till talk about in there, any-how?"

"Baseball," he said. "And movies."

"You talk about movies? What movies?"

"He likes Alfred Hitchcock. But mainly, we talk about baseball. The Braves. Eddie Mathews."

"That's what you talk about? Eddie Mathews?"

"And Spahnie," he said. "But yeah, he says Eddie

Mathews is the greatest guy in the National League."

"I like hearing you talk about our team," she said.

"Yeah, it's great to have a good team." With that, he escaped upstairs to his room.

———

The next day Uncle Till's prediction came true exactly as described. A heavy man in a dark gray suit emerged from nowhere as Keith was mooning along as though going nowhere in particular, a posture intended to disguise his progress toward the vacant lot. This weed-choked desolation where overgrown bricks lay scattered around a fire-blackened tree stump, where creeper vines matted the chain-link fence at its far end, and where an agile boy could squeeze into a half a dozen little hideaways, lately had colonized his imagination: When he was not celebrating the miracle of Uncle Till, he daydreamed about sliding on his belly through the Queen Anne's Lace outside his little portals, scanning the undergrowth for prey.

Keith was so intent on getting to the destination

he was pretending not to have that when the cop stepped in front of him, he acted as though the unknown man was an impediment like a garbage can and tried to dodge around him.

A huge hand clamped his shoulder. A deep voice said, "Hold on a second there, son."

Startled, the boy looked up into a wide, heavily seamed face with an almost lipless mouth and eyes like blue marbles set deep in dark, cobwebby sockets. "Uh," he said, and tried to scramble out of the man's grip.

The big hand tightened on his shoulder and pulled him back into place.

"You're Keith Hayward, aren't you?"

"Yeah?"

"I'm not keeping you from anything, am I? No important appointments, no girlfriend waiting to be taken out on a date?"

Keith shook his head.

"We're gonna get along real good. Because I'm pretty sure that's true, I'm gonna take my hand off your shoulder, Keith, and you're going to stay right there and talk to me, aren't you?

"Okay," Keith said, and the hand released him.

The man's rusty-looking smile contradicted all the rest of his face.

"My name is Detective Cooper. Cops like me, we're the good guys, Keith. We keep people like yourself and your family safe from the scum of society that might hurt them if we're weren't around. Do you have any idea what I want to talk about with you?"

A vivid image flooded his mind. He thought, *I kicked that cat into the fence and then I grabbed it by the neck and shoved the carving knife into its belly.*

"I don't think so."

"It's important you tell me the truth, Keith. Policemen always know when a person is lying. Especially detectives. Maybe I wasn't clear enough. So let me ask you this, Keith. Is anybody staying in your house? Someone not in your immediate family?"

Keith said nothing.

"I mean, someone not your mother or your father? Maybe related to you, though?"

"No," Keith said.

"I don't think you're telling me the truth, Keith.

You *know* you're lying to me. Let me tell you something. This is for your own good, and I want you to think about it. Lying to a policeman is a serious crime. If you do it, you can get in big trouble. *Big* trouble. So let's give it another try, all right? You do the right thing, I'll forget all about how you lied to me. Okay?"

"Okay." Detective Cooper fascinated Keith. He was carrying on as though kindness and patience were characteristic of him, but it was all an act, a performance, and not a very convincing one.

"The whole reason I'm here is that I want to talk to your uncle Tillman. People call him Till, which wouldn't make me too happy, but I guess it's fine with him. Till lives in Columbus, Ohio, but nobody's seen him around there for about a week and a half. I bet Till's camping out in your house. He's there right now, isn't he? If you tell me the truth this time, Keith, I'll make sure you won't have any trouble with the law."

"I didn't do anything!" Keith burst out. "Nobody said I was in trouble until now!"

Cooper's transparent duality, the thin folksy surface over the merciless granite of his actual self, frightened Keith more than what he was saying. The detective's inner self seemed to be swelling up, growing larger and larger, threatening to engulf the outer man. In seconds, his head would be two feet wide, and he would cover the entire sidewalk, still uttering these meaningless reassurances.

A hand closed around his arm and dragged him into the shade of a dying elm. Once they got out of the light, Cooper let go of his bicep and began patting his back. "Everything's going to be fine, kid. Nobody's saying you're in trouble. You can stop worrying."

Slowly, the moment of surreal panic faded, leaving Cooper an ordinary man, not a hideous inflating flesh-balloon. Keith's duties and ambitions came back to him.

"Are you all right, Keith? Take a minute. Settle down."

"I'm all right," the boy said. "I always was all right. Why are you talking to me that way?"

"You looked like you were going to cry on me, Keith. I'm on your side, son, you have to understand that. And I think I know why you wanted to cry."

"I didn't want to cry." *You're not like this, you're a fake,* he thought. Then, *Maybe I do want to cry.*

"Well, I think you did. And do you know what I think is the reason?"

You already told me why, Keith thought, and Detective Cooper filled the silence that followed with precisely the words the boy expected to hear.

"You don't like lying to me, I know that about you, Keith. You want to tell me the truth, but you're afraid I'll hurt your uncle. But I just want to talk to him. That's all, son. And if I talk to him, maybe I can even help him."

Even in the midst of his fear, all that one would expect in a twelve-year-old boy abruptly confronted with a massive policeman, the absurdity that a man whose face suggested nothing so much as a dull knife thought he could help Tillman Hayward made him want to laugh.

"Let's do it one more time, Keith. Way down inside you, you want to do tell me the truth. Uncle Till's hiding out in your house, isn't he?"

"No," Keith said. "He isn't staying with us. I wish he was, though, because then we could talk about baseball. Uncle Till loves Eddie Mathews, and so do I."

"Eddie Mathews," Cooper said.

"If you're so sure he's there, why don't you come into my house and look around for him? Check the closets, go down into the basement, look in back of the furnace?"

"Keith, I wish I could, I really do. But the law won't let me. Your uncle doesn't want anyone to see him, does he?"

"My uncle likes all the Braves," Keith said. "We used to talk about Warren Spahn, because he thinks Warren Spahn is really neat."

Detective Cooper thrust his face down into Keith's. The rusty smile was gone, and his eyes had turned the color of dry ice. A sharp, flamelike wave of terror seared the boy's lungs and throat.

"Thank you for your cooperation, Keith. And on a personal note. Just let me say this. I think you have the right to know that you are undoubtedly the ugliest kid it has ever been my privilege to meet. That *is* the truth, Keith. You are one ugly-lookin' boy. Puke on the sidewalk is handsomer than you. If they gave out trophies for terrible faces, you'd win every time. No girl is ever going to go out with you, Keith, you're never gonna get married, you're never even gonna pick a girl up, because every time you try, she'll run away screaming."

Detective Cooper straightened up, spun out of the shade, and disappeared into the downpouring sunlight that bounced off the hoods of cars, windshields, and glittery flecks of mica in the sidewalk.

Keith was not sure he could still walk. He felt as though the massive, gray-faced old policeman had cut off his legs at the knees. The streaks on his face had turned cool before he realized he was crying. Only after he had dragged his sleeve across his face did he think he could continue on his way down the block. When he came to the vacant lot, he kept on walking until he came to Sherman Boulevard, where he aimed himself like a guided missile at the abandoned building Uncle Till had summoned into his mind.

1962–1963
—

MILLER HAD A FIRST NAME, TOMEK, BUT NO ONE ever used it. Most people did not even know what it was. Even in grade school, where he had been a friendless victim, he had been just "Miller," as in, "Miller, get down and lick my spit off the playground," or "Miller, what makes you think I'm going to let you live through this here day?" Against all the odds, his life improved in high school, at least temporarily, because in December of his freshman year, he acquired a friend. Unfortunately, that friend was Keith Hayward.

Until the day when he rescued his comrade-to-be from a typical degradation, Keith himself had been basically friendless himself, though not so spectacularly as Miller. The unattractiveness remarked upon by Detective Cooper had, if anything, deepened during the four years since their encounter, and at the time in question was enhanced by a virulent breakout of acne that sprouted pustules, many of them visibly oozing, from every pore available upon his narrow forehead and flat cheeks. Unless they possess a blazing wit, great social skills, or an unusual degree of self-awareness, the truly ugly tend to have a difficult time in high school. Keith of course possessed none of these, yet he had never been a victim. He owned the secret weapon of his real self, which he hoarded and sheltered and allowed out of its private enclosure only for the purposes of pleasure and self-protection. Pleasure could be sought in the private room he had created beneath the abandoned diner on Sherman Boulevard;

self-protection occurred at those moments when some bully decided to turn him into a victim like Miller. At those moments, Keith did neither of the two things that born victims fall back upon. He did not look down and fall into silence, and he did not shrink away, hoping for mercy. Instead, he marched squarely up before his would-be tormentor, stared into his eyes, and said something like, "If I were you, I'd back away right now." The actual words were not important. What affected the bullies, who one and all actually did back away from him, was the expression they saw in his eyes. They could not have defined or described it, but it let them know that the smaller and seemingly pitiable boy before them knew more than they about the administration of pain. He enjoyed it more than they, and in a different way. In that area, he had no limitations, none.

By the beginning of his sophomore year, what lay behind Hayward's resolution had earned him a growing reputation for potential danger among his fellow students, although the faculty and staff at Lawrence B. Freeman High School never became aware that slinking down their hallways and unobtrusively carving on their desks was a true wild card. Most of Keith's teachers felt pity for him; the administration knew only that Hayward had maintained both a 2.75 grade point average and an absolute indifference to clubs.

And Hayward, who had barely noticed Miller's existence, did not so much as know his name on the day in early December when he walked into the boy's restroom and saw what the principal called "an unhappy situation" in the arena between the urinals and the sinks. Five or six seniors were clustered around a younger boy kneeling on the floor tiles. One of the juniors had been speaking to the boy, but at the moment he became aware of Hayward he shut his mouth and turned his head to glare at the intruder.

The boy next to him, Larry Babb, whom Keith knew slightly, said, "Get out, Hayward."

"No," Keith said, and in a moment of astonished silence walked past the boys to get to the stalls.

"What did you say?" the disbelieving Babb finally asked.

"I don't give a shit what you guys do. Just go ahead and do it."

"Aw, fuck you," Babb said, watching him home in on the second stall.

Instead of going in and locking the door behind him, Hayward turned around, leaned against the jamb, and crossed his arms over his chest, evidently settling in to enjoy the spectacle. "What are you going to do, kick him around?"

The boy who had fallen silent when Hayward came in turned his head back to regard Babb. "You *know* this pimply asshole?"

"His name is Hayward," Babb said, as if that were enough.

"Hayward? Who's *Hayward?*"

"He's a year behind us."

"I know, you were gonna piss on him," Hayward said.

"Get rid of him, Babb," said the evident leader, whose name later turned out to be Tolbert "Rocky" Glinka.

Larry Babb cast him a "why me?" glance. When this had no effect, he swiveled toward Hayward and let his face drop into an expression of weary authority. "You heard Rocky," he said. "Get out of here while you can still do it yourself."

"You were. You were actually going to piss on this kid." Hayward grinned at Babb, then, over his shoulder, at Rocky Glinka. "Real bunch of hot rods here, hey?"

"Whatever that's supposed to mean," said Glinka. "Larry?"

Babb moved toward Hayward, trying to look so menacing that the smaller, pimple-infested boy would take off before he had to touch him.

Smiling, Hayward stepped up directly in front of him. He put his hands in his pockets. Babb noticed that he smelled a little off, like something left too long in the refrigerator.

"You were going to take your dick out in front of this kid and show it to your buddies?"

"Go away," Babb said.

"I'm gonna stick around and watch. I don't think *you're* gonna stop me, are you?" He was staring straight into Babb's increasingly uncertain eyes.

The other boy glanced away and stepped back. "I don't care what you say, you fucking freak."

"*What?*" yelled Glinka.

"You can do what you want, but I'm getting out of here," said Babb. "The bell's going to ring in about five seconds."

"So what?"

"Go on, give 'em the big show," Hayward said.

The boy who was huddled on the floor began to weep.

"Miller, you got lucky, but it ain't gonna last for either one of you." Glinka parade-marched out of the bathroom, and his entourage followed.

Over the hubbub in the hallway, Glinka could be heard saying, "Will you assholes stop *chuckling?*" The sound of boys' voices drifted down the hallway and was replaced by the usual between-bells din of pounding feet, shrieking laughter, and locker doors slamming shut.

The boy kneeling on the bathroom floor was not at all part of the usual picture. His head touched the floor, and he was crying. The position of his head made his tears run sideways across his temples and slide into his hairline. He also appeared to be repeating some simple phrase over and over, although his voice might have been emanating from a jack-o'-lantern left outside in the weather since Halloween.

"You'll have to do better than that," Keith said, and moved around the boy to step up to the cracked porcelain wall, unzip, fish himself out, and, with a groan of pleasure, let loose. Hayward always enjoyed urinating, the touching, the unaccustomed exposure, the release of accumulated pressure. He thought his penis probably enjoyed the attention he gave it at such times, and sometimes, as now, when the stream had dribbled out, it seemed intent on proving him right. This time, he understood, his arousal came not from the usual sources but from the now comprehensible, though still mushy, words uttered by the freshman boy whose backward-pointing feet and lowered butt he could see by turning his head and looking sideways. The kid was bent over like a Muslim on a prayer rug. In a voice ragged and soft with exhaustion, he was saying," Oh thank you, oh thank you, oh thank you . . . I *hate* it when they piss

on me . . . thank you, oh thank you, oh thank you."
To that he added what sounded like the word "Sir."

"My name is Keith, okay?" Keith shoved himself
back into his pants. The groveling freshman continued to mutter behind him.

"Stop doing that," he said. "And get up, will you?
If someone walks in, we'll both be in trouble." He
kept facing the urinal to hide the bulge in his
trousers.

"Okay," the boy muttered. "I just wanted you to
know that I'm really grateful. Getting pissed on is
terrible. You have to go home and change your
clothes, and everybody knows what happened. Um,
my name is Miller."

At last he heard the sounds of Miller scrambling
to his feet. "How many times has that happened to
you?"

"Just once before. Well, twice. Only the first time
it was just Rocky, and I was in a ditch."

"So I guess that hardly counts."

"He pushed me, and I fell down. Rocky hates me.
But just about everybody hates me." There was a
pause. "Why are you looking away?"

Unable to prolong the moment any longer, Keith turned around. His erection, which had lost some of its urgency, still raised a lump alongside his fly.

The small, weedy, milk-white boy before him had hunched shoulders, big hands that dwarfed his wrists, and limp black hair that looked dead. His eyes and his nose were too large for his face, and his whole being looked cringing and elfin. The protuberant eyes skittered off Keith's pustular face, moved to the bulge at his crotch, then slid panicked into the middle distance.

"They were afraid of you," Miller said. "Rocky and them." Dangling from their spindly wrists, his swollen-looking hands were trembling.

"Doesn't mean you have to be."

"Okay," Miller said. "You won't piss on me, will you? I don't think you will."

"Definitely not today." The forlorn expression on Miller's face made him laugh. "That was a joke. Hey, I'd like to hear you thank me for saving you from Rocky and his buddies."

"But you told me to stop."

"That's when you were all bent over on the floor,

and you couldn't even talk right. I want you to thank me now, when you're standing up."

"Thank—"

"Hold on, Miller. *And*. I want you to thank me by doing something for me."

The boy's adam's apple jerked up and down. "The bell shoulda rung already."

"Be my friend," Keith said.

"Sure," said Miller, amazed. "I don't have any friends."

"Me, too. So we can be friends, you and me. Right? Only, I rescued you from those guys, so you owe me."

"How long has your face been like that?"

He was trying to change the subject, but both boys knew what was involved, and in a sense they had already agreed upon the terms of their contract.

"Because you were two years ahead of me at Townsend School, and back then you didn't look like that."

"The dear old days of Townsend. How did I ever miss you?"

"You want to know what? In about a year, maybe

less, you're gonna look different. The same thing happened to my brother. His whole face was one big zit. When they went away, he just had these little scars."

"You have a big brother? How old is he?" Hayward thought for a second. "Is he in this school?"

Miller gulped air. "He isn't in any school. My brother's dead. My dad got him drunk, and he died. His name was Vatek. Now my dad's in prison, and my mom won't let me see him."

"Where do you live?"

"Thirty-three fifty-five Auer."

It was only a few blocks from his own house. "On the way home, I want to show you a certain room," he said, and from his pocket produced a giant ball of keys.

It was in this fashion that Keith Hayward acquired the boy known as Miller.

———

After an initial period of fearfulness, then a week or so of despair, the hunched, spavined little creature with outsized eyes and hands that looked liked protuberances had learned at least in some fashion to enjoy Keith's private room. There were weekends when he puttered around with the animal heads and tails, the resilient paws and the scabby, shriveling skins, like a child set loose among his toys. When busy with his various "projects," Hayward occasionally glanced over at the other boy and smiled like a fond parent at the intricate movements through which the clumsy hands guided his trophies. Of course Hayward was not Miller's parent, but his Master.

Miller learned to resign himself to the sexual duties his role imposed upon him, but in the process he learned also that his Master was sexually excited by the craven and the cringing, by abjection and piteousness, precisely the tactics to which he attributed his survival into his freshmen year of high school. To save himself from tedious stretches laboring over his Master's "tool," which was in any case much smaller than his own, Miller attempted to change some of his behaviors and appear more confident. These efforts had some limited success. By May, during the long hours the boys spent in Keith's secret chamber, he was spending less time as a sex toy and more as a kind of assistant curator who helped arrange the trophies and exhibits.

They had begun to work with the numerous notices for lost cats and dogs that appeared so frequently in the neighborhood. In the beginning, Keith had ordered Miller to rip these posters off the walls and lampposts where they had been put up and throw them away, but near the end of winter, he realized that they could display the posters beside the remains of the pets they described. Matching the dead animals to their owners' drawings and word-portraits proved remarkably easy, although at times the fuzziness of the distinction between "marmalade" and "tabby" drove Keith half-mad with fury. If they had properly matched the posters with the cat and dog remains, there *were* some tabbies with fur the color of orange marmalade, almost a reddish tinge to the hair, but in most cases the animals might have been twins, and the owners just called them what they liked. In any case, the notices and cat skins that covered the walls of Keith's room made it look a bit like a grotesque museum. The

hides and heads of small animals and the mimeo-
graphed pieces of paper with boldfaced names hung
in three long, straight lines down the walls at the
sides of the room. Keith found this arrangement
beautiful.

It pleased Keith that Miller had instantly understood the necessity to maintain the sacred chamber
in an orderly fashion, and he was grateful to his
creature for having solved a problem that had grown
more serious with each fresh acquisition and might
have led, over time, to unwelcome intrusions upon
his territory. This was the question of disposal.
Keith's work involved the accumulation of a growing
pile of what he called "gizzards," the internal organs,
lungs and hearts and livers and bowels, as well as
several other small, wet body parts that he had never
identified. Before Miller had been introduced to his
room, Keith was in the habit of dumping whatever
he had left over—sometimes nearly an entire cat or
dog—into a big tin bucket left behind by the ban-
ished cult. After every two or three procedures, he
poured the messy leftovers into grocery bags pilfered
from a kitchen drawer, then carried the stained

(often dripping!) bags through the streets to the vacant lot at the end of his block. There he pushed the bags into the corner by the wall and did his best to cover them with dirt. Rodents and vermin made a swift job of eliminating most of the evidence.

The first time Miller had observed this process, he ventured, all but trembling with the awareness of his terrible audacity, that perhaps he might suggest a neater and on the whole less risky way of managing the problem of disposal. What was that? his Master demanded. Miller had a *suggestion*? By all means, let us hear it.

Quivering, Miller mentioned a stack of old newspapers in a broom closet and reminded his Master that *Joe's Home Cooking*, the restaurant two buildings down Sherman Boulevard, kept a row of metal garbage cans lined up in the alley. If they maybe wrapped the gizzards in newspaper and stuffed the parcels into the garbage cans, wouldn't that provide a neat, efficient solution to their problem?

Keith liked the way Miller talked. He never said anything the way you expected him to. He talked like a grown-up, but he was never vague or confusing. Miller spoke with tremendous clarity. The best part was the way he kept surprising Keith with the stuff he came up with. Once Keith asked him if he liked what they did with the cats and dogs, and Miller said that he had a few reservations, but it was a lot better than being beat up and pissed on over and over.

"Didn't your parents ever call the school and complain?"

"We don't complain," Miller said. "My parents have very strong foreign accents, and any kind of authority frightens them. They think they have to be submissive when dealing with real Americans."

About half of the other kids Hayward knew might be capable of offering such an analysis, but none of them would be able to articulate it so clearly. You had to be smart to use language that way. The more time that Keith spent with Miller, the more he realized that with only a little bit of work, his creature, his only friend, could easily do very well at school. Yet Miller puttered along on B minuses, Cs and Ds, exactly the grades he desired, neither so glittering nor so shameful as to attract attention. He never did homework, and Keith suspected that at times he deliberately gave wrong answers on tests. His principal goal in life appeared to be to slip beneath the radar and escape or avoid notice. For different reasons Keith felt much the same way.

Over the course of his freshman year, Miller grew more and more to value the circle of protection and safety that Keith Hayward created for him. The price of that magic circle, always distasteful, became less onerous and more merely habitual, over the winter and spring.

At school, and during his walks to and from Lawrence B. Freeman High School, Miller almost daily experienced the benefits his efforts earned for him. Rocky Glinka had threatened to punish both Keith and Miller for his humiliation in the boys' bathroom, and for a month Miller trembled in fear whenever he caught the crude, stupid bully sneering at him in the hallways, but nothing ever came of the threat. With Babb at his side, Glinka once spotted Hayward rummaging in his open locker, swept down on him, spun him around, and tried to ram him into the small, unusually crowded space. Something about the atmosphere within Hayward's locker made him feel threatened. He wanted to back away and get out of there, fast. At the same time, he also wished to pound Hayward senseless and close him up in his locker. Still holding his enemy by the biceps, Glinka moved a half inch away and shook his head. What was it? A kind of smell?

"Take your hands off me and move away," Hayward said.

Glinka raised his head and looked into Hayward's eyes, hoping to renew his energy and purpose. It was like looking into a cave. Glinka dropped his arms and stepped back. "What's in there, anyhow? Is your locker full of hair?" This was pure bravado.

"No," Keith said, and slammed his locker shut.

"Something *looked* at me," Glinka said, getting closer to his actual state.

Keith turned to Larry Babb, who had been hovering at his friend's shoulder. "Take him away, Larry. Get him out of here."

"You're a freak," Babb said, and did what he was told. No one at that school ever again bothered Keith Hayward or his friend, the boy called Miller.

Keith's life improved in one other significant way, too. By May of his junior year, Keith's face had almost entirely cleared up, so if he were not (nor ever could be) good-looking, he had anyhow ceased to be the kind of a walking suppuration in those days called a "pizza face." Many of the little knifelike scatter of scars that his acne had bequeathed him bent sideways and folded themselves into the long vertical furrows that already divided his cheeks. A little while later, his uncle told him that if he ever went bald, he might wind up looking liked the guy in that painting, *American Gothic*.

DECEMBER–JANUARY
1964–1965

CHRISTMAS WAS THREE WEEKS AWAY, AND WHILE with part of his mind Keith pondered what to give his uncle, Miller labored over his naked body. As sometimes happened, in the course of their exertions Miller had himself become excited, and due to the position he had taken over his master's body, for the first time in their relationship the evidence of Miller's arousal hung near his master's face. Keith could not admire his own erection without looking past the daunting organ swaying before his eyes.

A clear drop of viscous liquid drooled out of Miller and swung down on a silver thread. Keith balled his right hand and punched the back of Miller's thigh hard enough to leave a bruise.

"Get off!"

Miller turned his head and started to scramble off the cot at the same time. His eyes were round with shock.

"Are you a fag?" Keith bellowed. "Because I'm not."

"A fag?" Miller slid off the side of the cot and landed on one hip. "I thought you wanted me to . . ."

"You're not supposed to get a big fruity *kick* out of it!" Keith pointed, and Miller looked down. "I don't want some faggot sucking on my dick, Miller. I'm supposed to be enjoying it, but you're not."

"It's funny," Miller said. "By and large, I don't, actually. I can't really tell you why I got hard this time. It *is* sex, though."

"It's supposed to be sex for me, Miller, not for you. I don't *want* to have sex with you, because I'm not a pansy. And what do you mean, you don't *actually* enjoy sucking my dick? Maybe it doesn't satisfy you, is that it?"

"I'm not supposed to be satisfied," Miller wailed. "You don't want me to be satisfied!"

"You got too fucking close!" Keith yelled at him.

Miller folded himself into a ball, shielding his head with his arms and his chest with his crossed legs. The offensive organ tried to contract into his body.

Keith slid off the table and batted the back of Miller's head. His slave began to groan, "Please please please don't hurt me I didn't know anything was wrong *please* Keith *please . . .*"

Keith's body responded to abjection in its typical manner. Hitting Miller again only made him feel even closer to orgasm. He placed his hand on his erection and gave himself the few rough up-and-down strokes that were all he needed.

"For God's sake, clean yourself up," Keith said.

As his slave crawled away toward the heap of filthy towels, a wonderful idea came to Keith Hayward. "I want you to meet someone."

Miller quivered.

"Don't worry," Keith told him. "My uncle Till is a very, very cool guy."

———

Before he entered high school, Keith had never bothered to wonder about the crimes Detective Cooper thought Tillman Hayward had committed. The air of genial lawlessness that surrounded his uncle seemed a sufficient explanation for police interest in his case. No doubt he had been responsible for hundreds of crimes, maybe more. Indifference to legal technicalities was part of his character. The way the man sauntered down the street, the way he slouched against his pillow with his hat on his head and his hand wrapped around three fingers of bourbon, the way he did practically everything would probably be seen as a violation of the proper order by someone like Detective Cooper. Some people, a lucky few, were born that way, and some of *them*, like his aunt Margaret Frances/Margot, managed to wriggle their way right up to the top of the world, where there was always enough money and you could have all the cars and clothes and good food you wanted. Wasn't that what everyone wanted?

When Keith speculated about specific crimes Uncle Till might have committed, he dared go no further than the assumption that his uncle had a "private" room wherein he, much like Keith in the last few years of grade school, dissected other people's pets. Beyond that, he could not think; beyond that lay an abyss.

All this time, the conversations in the backyard and the extra bedroom, which had been the best conversations of his life, coiled through his mind like smoke, now and then shining with meanings that in seconds melted away. He felt as though he stood trembling before a great dark door, too terrified even to reach out his hand. Keith had never seen the Alfred Hitchcock movie his uncle loved, for *Shadow of a Doubt* was too old for the cinemas and too disturbing to be shown during the family hours on network television.

During his grade-school years, Keith's self-absorption kept him from noticing much the newspaper and radio stories about the Ladykiller. Perhaps for his sake, his parents avoided conversations about the murders and switched channels and radio stations when the subject came up. Keith knew that someone was killing women, three or four of them a year, over intervals wide enough for him to forget about the murders. Although at times he wondered what sort of man the killer might be, these speculations soon darkened to opacity, as if unwelcome in his mind.

Uncle Till slid into town at long intervals, never twice by the same mechanism. If one time he drove up in an unfamiliar car, the next he would arrive by train, or at the bus station. Another time, he claimed to be short of cash and to have traveled the entire distance on his thumb. He arrived in new cars, borrowed cars, cars temporarily left to him by traveling friends.

Not until he was seventeen and a high school junior did Keith realize that the Ladykiller had chosen to murder two Milwaukee women during a period when his uncle had returned to the old spare room alongside the kitchen. This recognition might never have come to him had he not strayed into a shop on his way home from school at the same time a delivery van dropped off tied-up bales of the *Milwaukee Journal,* the evening newspaper. On his way in, Keith glanced at the most prominent headline atop a stack that had just finished rolling across the sidewalk. *LADYKILLER CLAIMS DOWNTOWN VICTIM,* it read. Beneath the headline, Detective Cooper's weary, ironbound face angled down in lamplight at a cobbled alley and a rumpled gray-white sheet from which protruded a pale, upturned hand. The story began:

Police have identified the Ladykiller's probable ninth victim as Lurleen Monaghan, 29, of 4250 N. Highland Avenue, a secretary in the trust department at the 1st Wisconsin Bank. Miss Monaghan's body was discovered by pedestrians in the alley behind the Sepia Panorama, a N. 3rd Street nightclub, at 2:20 this morning. According to Homicide Detective George Cooper, the body had been moved to the alley after death.

"The Ladykiller murdered the victim in a private location and dumped her here, in back of a busy nightclub, where she was quickly discovered,"

said Detective Cooper. "Wednesday of last week, he followed the same procedure with the body of Laurie Terry. This monster is rubbing our faces in his crimes. Let me put this guy on notice. We are pursuing a number of active leads which will soon lead to his capture."

Keith continued on into the store, thinking only that it was strange that he had managed to stay essentially unaware of this villain's existence. The discovery of Laurie Terry's body had missed him altogether—and so would have this new outrage, had it not bounced up right before him. Now that the phrase had been placed in front of his eyes, he understood that he had after all heard of the Ladykiller. The phrase had entered his consciousness, but only barely. What struck him as strange was that this was precisely the sort of thing he thought he could find ... *irresistible*, however greatly his parents would object to his interest.

On the other hand, Detective Cooper, that meaty piece of shit, had not neglected to leave a wide, greasy trail across his memory.

A pad of thumbtacks slipped into his coat pocket. Without breaking stride, Keith moved up the aisle, extended an arm, snapped up a pot of glue, and dropped it into the other coat pocket. He had entered the five-and-dime on Sherman, in the same block but across the street from his sacred place, his church, his theater, to acquire, ideally without payment, some items useful to him. Recently he had become aware that he could make good use of a hammer, also of a metal file, also of any kerosenelike solvent akin to that employed by his father in the spray room at the can factory, and after he had pocketed a roll of tape he headed toward the back corner where he thought he remembered seeing a little hardware section. The solvent or kerosene or whatever it was would probably be difficult to find, but you never knew. It might turn up right in front of him, like Miller. Or like the bundled newspapers that had greeted him outside the little store.

And from that wandering thought came . . .

Without even faintly trying, Hayward recognized the meshing of two separate calendars, his uncle's and the murderer's. Laurie Terry had met her death late the previous Wednesday, the day Tillman Hayward had surprised his Milwaukee family by calling from the bus station to tell his brother's wife hello, my dear one, here I am, no worries, I'll get to the house on my own. Twenty minutes later, she had gone to the front window to see, on the far side of a great snow bank, her brother-in-law getting out of a strange woman's car just in time to twirl his suitcase from the back seat and into the arms of his devoted nephew, who was arriving home from another deadly day at Lawrence B. Freeman. Together, Tillman and Keith came up the path through the snow, already deep in conversation.

They had talked long and often since that moment, but never, Keith now saw, of actual murders—murders of human beings. Here was the great dark door before which he had quailed; here was the true, the real abyss. And as he stood before it, the door swung open, and the abyss yawned wide. Lit with bright, wandering fires, his entire body seemed to tremble from within. A great confirmation rang through him and seemed to lift him off the ground.

His head reverberated. For a moment he was conscious of nothing but his blood coursing through his brain and body in a continuous, racing stream. Then his knees went rubbery, and he began to slip toward the floor.

A female voice called, "Sir! Are you all right?"

It was like being pulled back to shore. His eyes cleared, and he found he could halt his descent. A woman with piled-up hair and cat's-eye glasses stood perhaps ten feet down the aisle, extending one hand and one foot as though poised between flight and approach. She had big freaky eyes, and her mouth was a beak. He could not permit this woman to place her hand on his coat.

"I'm fine," he managed to croak.

"It looked like you almost fainted."

"Well, *something* happened," he admitted. "But it's over." He straightened his spine, rolled his head back, and inhaled. Uncle Till, seated cross-legged on the spare bed with his hat on his head, a playing card in one hand, dark smiling eyes taking him in . . .

Oh, tonight I think I'll just wander around, see if anything interesting turns up.

Who was the dame with the car? Just another dame with a car, nephew.

"Can I get anything for you?" She still held the posture of a bird coming in for a water landing.

"No, I was just looking for . . ." Keith tried to think to think of something small and affordable. "A notepad?"

"Aisle two." The woman slowly pulled herself upright. She lowered her arms gave him an uncertain smile. "I ought to get back to the register."

. . . wander around, see if anything interesting turns up.

Keith smiled back at her.

"Why, you're just a boy," the woman said. "I don't know how I could have thought—"

"I'll get that notebook," Keith said, and turned around slowly, wondering why he had not asked about files or hammers. Wondering, too, what age she had thought him. He had to go home, he had to talk to Uncle Till.

Could you have a conversation like that? One that acknowledged the great open door and the shimmering license that lay beyond it? Or were such conversations conducted in the silences be-tween ordinary words and phrases? With the sense of standing on the lip of a great precipice, Keith rushed down the last aisle past displays of ribbons, pins, elastic bands, and buttons on long cards, see-ing nothing.

His uncle Till was the Ladykiller. Like a general or a great monarch, he had led his forces out into a dark, unknown territory, and seized control of all that lived there. His bed was a throne, his hat a crown. And his scepter . . .

. . . *I don't know how they'd do it, but for sure, if it was* me, *I'd use a knife.*

Just before he sped through the shop door, he glanced sideways at the woman with the weird hair and could not refrain from twisting his mouth into something like a smile. He did not know if it was meant for a taunt or reassurance, and it felt like nei-ther. Instead, it felt like the ghost of an emotion—a gesture to an unknown force. The hesitant face under the tortured hair displayed sympathy and curiosity. Then the woman's face hardened with suspicion, and she began to rise from her stool. Keith Hayward and his ghost of a smile had already fled into the cold and snowy street.

When he got back home, he raced through the business of dragging his boots off his feet and shedding his heavy coat and unwinding his scarf and pulling off his cap and transferring his stolen goods to his pants pockets and hanging up everything else. Then, finally, he could pass through the door to the kitchen, where his mother, engaged in an unruly shelf paper project, turned from the cabinets and a rank of plates of various sizes to look him over, make sure his shoes were civilized, and ask him about school. His response, as always noncommittal and vague, should have satisfied her, but instead of turning back to the shelf and the long curl of paper, she said, "What's going on with you, Keith?"

"What? Nothing. Why."

"You seem excited. You're all wound up inside. Tight as a watch spring."

"I guess I'm a *little* excited, Mom," he said. "Mr. Palfrey gave me a B+ on my *Grapes of Wrath* paper."

She cocked her head and smiled, mechanically.

The smile vanished. "You didn't have anything to do with the Rodenkos' cat, I hope. Mrs. Rodenko was talking to me about it for half an hour the other day. It's been a week, and she's worried sick."

Keith put on an affronted, wounded look. "The Rodenkos' *cat*? Mom, are you still worrying about that time you saw me doing something dumb? I was twelve years old, Mom. I was a kid. You *know* Uncle Till talked to me all about that. Jeez."

The hide of the Rodenkos' cat, an odorous, hissing monstrous creature either marmalade or tabby, hung on the wall of the secret room beside the pathetic poster the Rodenkos had taped to lampposts and billboards.

"Sometimes I wonder about you and my husband's brother," she said.

"What?"

"Just lately, I don't know . . . Does he tell you what he does when he goes out at night?"

"Mom, he sees people. He has dates. You know."

"Oh, I know. Yes. I do." She looked down at her hands, then cast a glance behind her at the stripped

71

shelves and the curl of paper. "At least that policeman stopped hanging around here, making me feel
like something was wrong. *Bad* wrong."

"All that was a long time ago, Mom."

"That man was very sure of himself. I *saw* him
once, out in the alley. He was trying to look through
our windows."

"He doesn't come around anymore."

"That doesn't mean something won't bring him
back."

Now Keith understood: his mother had been
reading the newspapers.

"You shouldn't worry about him, Mom. Don't let
yourself get carried away."

She smiled. "That's what your father says."

Keith forced himself to smile back.

His mother said, "You look more relaxed than you
did when you came in."

"You do, too," he said. "Uncle Till's here, isn't he?
Is it all right if I go see him?"

"Don't make a nuisance of yourself."

She waved him off and turned back to her work.
Keith went out of the kitchen and stood before his

uncle's door. For a second he shocked himself by wondering if he should knock, if he should speak, if he should go ahead. Uncertain, he stood before the immensity of the choice that faced him. Stay or go? Speak or leave in silence? For one thing, he had just realized for the first time that his mother might be able to hear whatever passed between his uncle and himself, but the choice went far beyond questions of privacy. Breathless, he raised his hand, and yet he hesitated, unable either to knock or walk away.

"Keith, is that you?" came his uncle's soft and rasping voice. "Come on in."

He lowered his hand, and was surprised that sparks did not leap from the knob. Turning it slowly, he heard the bolt slide into the plate.

"Good boy," the voice whispered.

Keith pulled the door fully open to reveal his uncle seated on his green blankets, his hat on his handsome head. Till had been reading a magazine but had turned to face the doorway, that he might regard whatever spectacle was unfolding there. He was smiling, and his eyes were alight. "You can do it," he whispered.

In full recognition of what he was doing, the boy came forward. Let this be said for Keith Hayward: when he came to the door, he entered his ruinous estate without hesitation. Once inside the room, he whispered back, "You *do* do it, Uncle Till."

"Oh?" Till's look of amusement deepened.

For the first time, Keith understood what sentimental authors meant when they spoke of falling into someone's eyes. Long and narrow to begin with, his uncle's eyes seemed to widen and enlarge with anarchic mirth. Tilden Hayward was irresistible: a satyr, a faun, a devil.

"Meaning what?" he said, softly.

In silence, Keith closed the door behind him. For a moment, he stood there with his hands folded behind his back. Here was another great threshold, and with only a second's pause, he crossed it to stand within two feet of his hero.

In a voice just above a whisper, Keith said, "Lurleen Monaghan." He searched his memory, and as a bear dips into a stream and snatches up a glittering fish, speared the second name. "Laurie Terry."

"Well, now." Till's amusement spilled over into

soft, chuckling laughter. "Laurie Terry, eh? Lurleen Monaghan, is that right?"

"I guess so." In fact, Uncle Till's response left no doubt as to his accuracy.

"How did you happen to learn those names, Keith?"

"The front page of the *Journal*."

Never taking his eyes off his nephew's, Uncle Till nodded, slowly, like a judge coming to a conclusion about a complicated legal point. "Our secret just got bigger, didn't it?"

"I guess *so*."

Till drew his head back a couple of inches. His eyes got narrower. Evidently he reached a conclusion about that complex matter. "Could be time I showed you my little place. What do you think?"

"I'd like that," Keith said.

———

After dinner, Till asked Keith's parents if it would be all right for him to take their son to a theater on the east side, the Oriental, to catch a screening of a movie they both wanted to see. It was *Charade*, with

Cary Grant and Audrey Hepburn, which one reviewer had called "the best Hitchcock movie Hitchcock never made."

"Leave me out," said Keith's father. "Cary Grant's a homo, and Audrey Hepburn looks like a praying mantis."

Keith's mother looked wistful, but asked only if Keith had any unfinished homework.

"I did it in study hall, Mom," he said, which was not entirely a lie. Shortly after dinner, uncle and nephew set off through a cold night glittering with stars.

———

Till led him past the vacant lot and around the corner, then down another long two blocks and around another corner before walking into the street and pulling out the keys to a long black Studebaker Keith had never seen before. Freezing inside his heavy coat, the boy waited for his uncle to get in and open the passenger door for him. The white clouds of his breath seemed to hang before him for an unusually long time, as if preserved by the cold. Although Uncle Till was wearing merely his hat, a sweater, and an unzipped leather jacket, he seemed to be unaffected by the temperature, even while blowing on his key to warm it.

"Aren't you cold?" Keith asked.

"Fact is, I like cold weather," his uncle replied. "Sharpens you up. In the heat, things get sloppy."

Till wound through the city until he got to Capital Drive, then drove straight west. Keith gazed out at neighborhoods and businesses he had never seen before, a ball bearing factory, an enormous shopping center, Roy Rogers and Arthur Treacher restaurants, a Howard Johnson's, a used-car lot with pennants like colored icicles and huge spotlights sending yellow-white beams into the black sky.

Finally they passed 100th Street, a straight, narrow line rolling past small, comfortable-looking houses down a low grade, then up another, steeper grade. 100th Street! Keith had no idea the numbers went up so high.

"Where is this place, anyhow?" he asked.

"You'll see."

"Is it far?"

"You'll see."

In a suburb called Brookfield, Till veered off Capital Drive and cut through streets lined with big
houses on wide, snowy lawns to Burleigh, where he
turned west yet again. Ten minutes later, a metal
sign advised them that they had entered the town of
Marcy, population 83. A wilderness of white fields
lay behind a narrow town hall, a frame house without windows, and an abandoned bar. Across the
street was a one-story grade school. The town
looked as though it had been stolen by aliens and set
down in a desolation. Uncle Till pulled in and
parked the car between the windowless house and
the shell of the old tavern. Keith got out and
watched his uncle tug his huge ball of keys out of his
pocket and, smiling, start flipping through them.

"I wanted to have a place out of town, see? Far
away from Detective Cooper."

Till held up a long, blunt key. "So I drove around
until I found this place." He nodded at the bar and
started walking toward it. "Nobody ever comes to
this side of the street, and the kids and faculty are all
gone after five o'clock."

"What about Columbus?" Keith asked. "You have a place there, too, right?"

"No—no—no—no. In Columbus, everything's completely different. *I'm* different. In Columbus, I have a wife and two daughters. They don't know anything about this, and they never will."

"Come on." Too astonished to move, Keith watched his uncle walk around the hood of the car. "You don't. You can't."

"Oh, but I can, I do. I recommend that you think about doing the same. We all have to make some sacrifices, after all."

Mouth open, Keith crunched across the gleaming snow to join his uncle at the door.

"But what do they think you do?"

"I own a bunch of apartment buildings. Well, my wife inherited them from her father, so actually we own them jointly."

"You're rich." This was astonishing.

"I'm comfortable. I never told your dad and mom because I wanted to be able to keep coming back here as a bachelor."

Silent, Keith watched his uncle slip the key into a

round metal lock newer than the door it protected.

"How can you keep coming to Milwaukee?"

"I'm looking for investment properties in my old home town. Let's get inside."

After relocking the door behind them, Till produced a small flashlight from an inner pocket of the leather jacket and played its beam over a dusty wooden floor, a long dark bar, and rickety-looking barstools. With Keith behind him, he set off past a rank of glum booths and ancient coat hooks. The air was frigid. When he came to a second, narrower door, he opened it, flipped a switch, and flooded the basement with bright fluorescent light. He started moving quickly down the stairs, and Keith followed, filled with wonder.

"Peace and quiet, comfort and security," said his uncle. At the bottom of the stairs, he looked up over his shoulder and smiled. "Behold."

While the ever-amazing Tillman Hayward wandered around turning on space heaters, Keith did as commanded and *beheld*. As clean as an operating theater, the long, wide basement contained two sparkling metal tables with drip trays, a shiny tile

floor dotted at intervals with drains, metal wall pan-
els hung with knives, saws, and hatchets, and on the
other side of the cement circle where the furnace
had stood, a back wall lined with green lockers, each
with a padlock. The rectangular windows set high in
the walls had been bricked over.

"Did it all myself," said Uncle Till, answering an
actual though unasked question. "If I'd hired work-
men, I would have had to kill 'em, and that was an
unacceptable level of risk. Took me over a year, but
now this place is pretty much the way I want it. The
heaters will take the chill off in a minute—they get
it up to about sixty degrees, which is warm enough.
In summer, it gets too damn hot down here, but all I
can do is plug in some fans."

"Amazing," Keith said.

"I have to admit, I'm kinda proud of what I was
able to accomplish here."

Keith walked up to a shiny metal table and
touched its leather wrist and ankle restraints.

"So you . . . ?" He let the crucial question hang.

"I put a little something in their drinks to cool 'em
out. Bring 'em out here, got plenty of duct tape over

in the cabinet, but nobody can hear 'em anyways. Lift 'em up on the tables and go to work. Before I start in, I strip off, hang up my clothes—plumbed in a little shower over there next to the lockers."

Keith's face and hands felt hot, and his heart was booming. "Do you screw them?"

Uncle Till grinned and laid a hand on his nephew's shoulder. In the shadow of the hat brim, his eyes looked molten. "You want to know if I fuck 'em, son? Hell, yeah. Most of the time, anyhow. And not just once, and not just in the one hole. Tell you the truth, nephew, sometimes I think I'd fuck a woodpile if I knew a body was in there. Wouldn't matter what kind, neither."

Not long after, they were driving back home through a world that looked both exactly the same and utterly transformed.

———

Two years later and three weeks before Christmas, under the same wintry skies, Keith Hayward at last realized that for the first time in his life he had it in his power to offer his uncle a gift that would actually be worthy of him. Because Tillman always returned to Ohio by the 17th or 18th of December, he knew he had about a week and a half to set things up. Keith's parents explained Till's pre-Christmas departure from their house as the result of his natural desire to spend the holiday with friends and intimates in Columbus, thought to be of a more sophisticated circle than any available to him in Milwaukee. To include Till in their modest family celebration, they exchanged gifts the day before his departure. Bill and Maggie always gave him things like socks or handkerchiefs, and he replied with gifts of a slightly more lavish nature, a bottle of expensive bourbon or a robe for his brother, a pretty scarf or blouse for his sister-in-law.

In the past, Keith's parents had always solved the problem of his gifts to his uncle by going to a shop called Notes & Notions, buying a cheap picture book about New England lighthouses or fancy cars or something similar, and wrapping it up with an attached card on which he had scrawled his name. Uncle Till, ever cool, always thanked him for these gifts and acted as though they interested him, but everyone understood that the photographs of Concord Point Light and Edgartown Light, of Bugattis and Dusenbergs, amounted to mere place-holders that would serve until Keith grew old enough to select gifts by himself. In December of 1962, that date was assumed still to lie in the future, and the place-holder, forty-eight pages of handsome yachts, had already been purchased.

Keith's real present could not be wrapped in Christmas paper and settled beneath the tree. On the afternoon of Friday the 14th of December, he ordered Miller to meet him in the secret room at seven o'clock the following evening. After a dinner during which the host's brother offered an hilarious, never-before heard account of his brief experience as a soldier in the United States Army, Keith followed his uncle back to the spare room and said he hoped Till would be free the next evening, because he had a surprise he wanted to give him.

"A surprise? That sounds interesting." Uncle Till was leaning toward a mirror, watching his hands wind a polka-dot necktie into a handsome half-Windsor knot.

"It's my Christmas present to you. The real one."

"Well, well." From the mirror, his eyes flashed an electric shock into his nephew's. "I gather this involves our private concerns."

"Yes."

"Let's be careful, then."

Till turned away from the mirror and slid his beautiful hands into his pockets. His head bent forward. For a moment, he regarded the scuffed-up sisal rug that covered the floor.

"You tell your parents that you're going to hang out with the famous Miller, and I'll just say I have to meet a friend. We leave separately, we come back separately. Does that work for you?"

"It's good."

"Where do you want to meet up?"

"At my place."

"Easy as pie. What time?"

"Seven."

"Seven it is. I'll say this for you, kid: you got me interested."

"What are you going to do tonight?"

"Gotta check my traps, boy, gotta check my traps."

Till's sudden grin caused him, if only for a second, to resemble a large, untrustworthy dog.

After a long séance before *The Alfred Hitchcock Hour* and *The Fugitive* on the TV, during which his mind could barely comprehend the action or dialogue, Keith assented to his mother's suggestion that he looked tired. It was only ten-thirty, half an hour before his usual bedtime. Sticking effortlessly to his own schedule, his father lay stretched out and lightly snoring in his lounge chair. In half an hour, Channel 12 was going to show *The Indestructible Man*, but his mother was right, he did feel oddly exhausted. However, when he put on his pajamas and slipped into bed, he discovered that he could not sleep.

Late in the night, he heard his uncle come in through the back door. Soft, light footsteps crossed the kitchen and passed into the spare room. A few minutes later, Till emerged to let himself into the downstairs bathroom and release a long, thunderous cascade of urine. He flushed the toilet and returned to his quarters. When silence returned to the ground floor, Keith switched on his bedside lamp and looked at his clock. It was three thirty. He fell asleep soon after.

Four hours later, he came downstairs in jeans and a warm flannel shirt, wandered into the kitchen to get something to eat, and found his mother seated at the table, exhaling cigarette smoke over both a bowl of Captain Crunch and an open copy of the morning paper, the *Milwaukee Sentinel*.

"Good morning, Mom," he said.

"Morning." She looked up from the paper and squinted at him. "You never get up this early on a Saturday. And you look as tired as an old dog. Why aren't you still in bed?"

He saw no reason not to tell her the truth. "I couldn't sleep any more."

"There's something wrong. What is it? You tell me right now, Keith."

"Mom," he said. "I just couldn't sleep." He turned from the table and began to rummage through the boxes in the cereal bin.

"That's not healthy."

Keith could feel her eyes on his back. He waited for whatever it would be.

"Is something going on with that Miller?"

A tingle of alarm passed through his nervous system. "No, Mom, nothing's going on. Not with Miller or anyone else."

"You want me to make you something for breakfast? It's no use waiting for your father, he won't be up for another two hours. And I don't blame him, don't think I do. He works long, hard hours, that man. If you ask me, his brother should be more like him."

"Dad wishes he was more like Uncle Till."

"Well, he shouldn't. Till is never going to marry a rich woman, he's just going to chase girls and stay up late in bars and pick up money whichever way he can. And I don't think you should be spending so much time with a man like that. Come away from that cereal and tell me what you'd like for breakfast."

He turned around and saw his mother taking him in as thoroughly as she could. She stubbed out her cigarette. "Well?"

"Scrambled eggs?"

"If your uncle didn't clean us out when he came in

last night." She stood up and went to the refrigerator. "Good. Plenty of eggs, plus some bacon. He even left us some orange juice." She took a half-gallon container of milk from the refrigerator and reached for a glass. "Sit down."

He sat. "I never saw you reading the paper before, Mom."

"If something terrible happens, I want to know."

"Oh."

"Things are going on you shouldn't even know about." She placed before him a glass of milk and a smaller glass of orange juice.

"In this paper?" Genuinely curious, he slid the paper a quarter-turn toward him and looked over the headlines. Most of them concerned local politics.

"No, thank goodness. Now give that paper back to me."

When she set his breakfast before him, the odors arising from the plate almost made him groan with hunger. Until that moment, he'd had no idea that he was ravenous.

"I don't think you should spend so much time with your uncle."

He shoveled a forkful of eggs into his mouth and added a two-inch bite of bacon.

"You're not going out with him again, are you?"

Around his food, he said, "Mom, it was just a movie."

"I don't care what it was, I don't want you doing it again."

He swallowed, struggling to keep his alarm under control. "Mom, what's wrong? Don't you like Uncle Till anymore?"

"Everybody likes him, that's the trouble. But I'm not saying I trust him, mind. And you shouldn't be tagging along behind him anymore. The world isn't as safe as you think it is, sonny."

Unable to reply to this absurdity, Keith forced himself to eat slowly. His mother joined him at the table, turned a page of the open newspaper and ran her eyes across the columns, then jumped up again to refill her coffee cup from the percolator. When she again took her chair, she lit another Kent.

"Tell you the truth, I'll be glad when he leaves in another few days. Your father worships that man so much, neither one of us ever stopped to think about what kind of influence he might be on you. Decent people don't live that way."

"There isn't just one way to be decent," he said.

There this conversation ended.

———

For the rest of the day, Keith did little but watch a parade of cartoons on television and meander around the house, waiting for Uncle Till to come out of the spare room. He flipped through the latest *Life*, which, no surprise, had a picture of the late President Kennedy on the cover. As Keith roamed through the magazine, he wondered how, in an entire extra-long issue devoted to the Kennedy assassination, a magazine thought to be so great could include only one lousy single article about Lee Harvey Oswald. He turned page after page about the dead president, many pages about Jackie Kennedy (whom Keith privately considered probably the most boring woman on earth), and a surprising number of pages dedicated to Lyndon Baines Johnson. There should have been much, much more about Kennedy's mortal antagonist, his opposite number. To make matters even worse, *Life* ran only a few pictures of the assassin, and he was the man who had made everything happen. Keith had lived long enough to understand that very few people even came close to sharing his point of view, but wasn't it obvious that this guy, Oswald, had more or less changed the rules? You could come up out of nowhere, you could appear to have led a misguided and wasted life, and yet all it took was a gun to place you on the same level as the President of the United States—if *he* was the most powerful man in the world, then you were *right beside him.* After a while, the refusal of influential Americans to recognize the amazing transformation Lee Harvey Oswald had created in their national life, to comprehend the actual revolution this former loser had brought about, made him feel so frustrated he could no longer bear to look at the magazine.

His uncle emerged only long enough to take a shower and walk, bathrobe flapping, into the kitchen to make a peanut butter and jelly sandwich. He took it back into his room and dined alone. While Keith numbed himself with *Rocky and Bull-*

winkle, Maggie Hayward cornered her husband, Bill, at the breakfast table, and in whispers and quiet words conducted what her son knew to be a tireless military campaign. Bill Hayward shook his head, he remonstrated, he protested, but as all the while he was also consuming the fried eggs, crisp bacon, warm buttered toast, and hot coffee his wife had prepared for him, it could be said that he had already capitulated and all his apparent countercampaigning amounted to mere smokescreen and misdirection. Maggie Hayward had changed her mind about her brother-in-law. She saw him in a new, unflattering light, and his days under her roof were numbered.

"Look, kid," Till said to him that evening, "it's crummy, but I understand it. Your mother saw the same newspaper you did, and it scared her a little. Maggie didn't want to think what came into *your* mind right away, and she doesn't, that's for certain, but something flickered in her noggin, and all of a sudden she thinks I'm a bum and a bad influence on you."

"I don't get it," Keith said. They were parked at a

meter on Sherman Boulevard. It was a few minutes before seven.

"Unlike you and me, most people hide their real motives from themselves. They have no idea why they do the things they do. Oh, they talk all day long about what made them do this and that, but what they tell you isn't even close to the truth. Because they don't *know* the truth. And why is that? They can't let themselves know it. The truth is unacceptable. Every human being on earth tells millions of lies in the course of his life, but most of those lies are to himself about himself. Your mother is a perfect example. Well, well. Could this be your buddy?"

Keith had already seen Miller's huddled form, hands in the pockets of his hooded coat and watch cap on his head, trudging toward them. His head was bent, his eyes fixed on the sidewalk.

"That's him," Keith said.

Miller plodded right up to the hood of the Studebaker. Without looking in, he swung sideways and darted into the shadowy space between the empty building and a long display window filled with television sets and washing machines. Soon he had disappeared into the darkness. According to the dashboard clock, it was exactly seven o'clock.

"He'll wait by the back door," Keith said. "Merry Christmas, Uncle Till."

"That kid is my present?" Till burst into soft laughter. "God damn. You're something else, you are. Keith, I am truly impressed."

The boy took this in with the warmth of a benediction: it was a blessing more paternal than any his father could have given him.

"Let me tell you one thing, sonny boy. You're going to do amazing things. Maybe no one will ever know about them. Doesn't matter."

Uncle Till patted Keith's left knee with his shapely and ungloved right hand, and the chill of his touch burned through to the skin.

"Fact is, it'd be better that way—if all your accomplishments are as secret as the room in there. But I'll know, somehow or other." Till's frozen grip tightened on Keith's knee and burned snow and ice straight into the bone. "I'll always know."

Keith could not imagine how his uncle was able to tolerate such coldness. Any moment, he would be forced to cry out. Then his uncle released him.

"Let's meet Miller," Keith said.

Uncle Till smiled at him. "In a second. Miller will wait. I'm happy to say that I have a present for you, too."

"You do?" Keith was stunned with pleasure.

"Open the glove compartment. Let me know what you find in there."

Keith pushed the button on the glove compartment and folded down its door. The inside light had burned out long ago, but visible atop the usual heap of maps and manuals lay a long, narrow white box bound with a red ribbon.

"A box," he said.

"A box? Well, get it out of the glove compartment and see what's inside."

With something like reverence, Keith removed the box, set it on his thighs and removed the ribbon. Then he raised the top of the box and lifted out a white bag. He already knew what his present was, and that it would be better of its kind than anything he had ever known.

"Oh boy," he said. "What's that word? Sabat – Sabateer."

"Sabatier," Till said. "You can't do better, I don't care what anybody says."

Keith drew the long knife from the bag and rested it across the palms of his hands. "Boy. Thanks."

"That's a chef's knife. You can use them for damn near anything, chopping, slicing, even deboning. Keep it clean and sharp, and it'll give you good service for years. For decades."

"Is this like the one you use?"

"Sure, I have a knife just like it," Till said. "In time, you'll have a whole collection. But your chef's knife, that's the centerpiece, that's your show pony. Do I have to tell you that you can't let your mother find it?"

"I won't even bring it home. I'll hide it in here."

Uncle Till cracked open his door. "What say we let poor Miller get in out of the cold?"

———

In seconds, they had slipped into the narrow passageway between the buildings. The sleeping washing machines in the enormous window gave way to grubby brick. Underfoot, empty beer bottles and crumpled cigarette packets lay upon a track of frozen earth a foot and a half wide. Inside the passage, the walls seemed five or six stories high. The chef's knife rode inside his belt at the small of his back, and it felt as though he had been carrying it there for months. Coming along steadily behind him, Uncle Till perfectly matched his pace. Then at last Keith burst out into the alley and saw Miller hunkered down in front of the back door, hugging his knees for warmth.

"I wondered if you were ever going to show up," Miller said. "It's too cold to make me wait out here."

Then he saw Till moving out of the shadows and, more quickly than Keith had ever seen him do anything before, jump to his feet. When Till moved up beside Keith and gave him a look of frank inspection, Miller folded his coat around him and tried to disappear into the bricks and mortar behind him.

"Whoa," he said. "What is this?"

"Didn't I tell you I had a surprise for you?" Keith asked.

"No," Miller said. He sounded resentful.

"Sorry. I thought I did. Well, it's a *wonderful* surprise, Miller. This man is my uncle. Uncle Till is the best teacher I ever had. I thought he deserved a really special Christmas present. So I'm giving you to him. You know what I think, Miller? I think you're in for a wild old time."

"This is going to work out just fine," said Uncle Till. "What are we waiting for?"

"I don't think this is a good idea," said Miller.

"Too bad."

"You can't give people as presents to other people."

"Not usually."

Keith pulled his ball of keys from his pocket and quickly located the one that unlocked the back door.

Still leaning against the brickwork, Miller was only a foot and a half to his left, both staring down and flinching away. His pores seemed to exhale an odd, metallic smell. Bronzy and unpleasant, it also floated from his open mouth. Beneath the hem of his winter coat, Miller's knees were jigging in his blue jeans. The smell was fear, Keith realized: fear was a physical property, and it stank.

"I wish you'da let Rocky Glinka piss on me," Miller whispered.

"At the time, you sang a different tune," Keith said, passing through the door. It was nearly as cold inside the building.

"You want me to piss on you, Miller?" Uncle Till sounded amused.

"Not really," Miller said. He followed Keith inside.

Till came in last and closed and locked the door behind them. "Because if you have any special requests, I could always fit them into my schedule."

In the darkness, Keith took a small Maglite from his coat pocket and played its beam across the floor until the circle of light centered on a new-looking Medeco lock about three inches across. "Hold this, will you?" he said, and passed the flashlight to Till, who kept it shining on the lock.

"Good work," Till said. "Yours is in the basement, too?"

"Just like yours."

Keith unlocked the Medeco, reached in, and flipped two switches that illuminated the basement and the rickety-looking wooden stairs leading to it. The treads creaked as he went down into the light.

Miller moved onto the first step and looked up over his shoulder.

"You can rest easy, kid," Till said. "I've never killed anyone with a dick, and I never will. Unless, you know, one day, I don't have any choice."

Downstairs on the cement floor, surrounded by the familiar animal hides and the posters for lost pets, Miller seemed less terrified. His knees no longer vibrated, but he kept shifting his eyes sidelong to glance at Till. His pallid face was stiff with fear. He asked the floor, "What are we going to do, exactly?"

"We're going to enjoy ourselves and experience life to the fullest."

"I see," Miller said, looking extremely unhappy.

"And for me to enjoy myself in the deepest possible way, nephew, I'm afraid that I really will have to be left alone with my Christmas present."

Miller's eyes flared at Keith.

"Are you sure about that?"

"Oh, yes, Keith, I am absolutely sure about that. That won't be a problem, I trust."

"It might be a problem for Miller."

"If Miller has a vote, it *is* a problem," said Miller. "A big one."

"Boy, I'd like to see you take your clothes off, so why don't you indulge me by doing that little thing?"

"It's cold down here," Miller said, but he shed his coat and began to unbutton his shirt.

"Pretty soon you won't notice that anymore," said Uncle Till. "Are you hung pretty good, kid?"

"I don't know," Miller mumbled.

"We'll find out soon enough. There's a lot of things we're about to find out, Miller." Till turned his face to Keith and raised his eyebrows.

"Oh!" Keith said. "Okay. Ah, there's a diner down the street, I'll get a coffee and some fries, or something."

"Try their cherry pie," said his uncle. "Fit for a king, that is."

Uncle Till looked like a king—*regal*, Keith

thought, with his head back and his perfect hands folded in front of his chest. He looked like a famous hunter Keith had once seen in a photo, posed with one foot on a dead lion in Africa.

"When should I come back?" he asked.

"An hour is all I'll need."

Keith nodded and turned toward the stairs. His last impression of Miller was of his comrade and slave shirtless and fish-white, shrinking into himself, his eyes dull and hopeless.

Upstairs, he left the basement unlocked and followed the beam of the Maglite to the rear door. Before he had let himself out, Keith heard Miller emit a sharp, high-pitched outcry, as if scalded. Before leaving for the diner, he turned the key in the back door's lock and heard the bolt snick safely home.

He set off a little bell when he went into the coffee shop, but nobody, not even the waitresses or counter staff, looked up. At the end of the counter, a fat man in a cloth cap and a dirty brown overcoat sat over a ham sandwich and a cup of coffee, reading the same issue of *Life* Keith had seen at home. Worn-out couples ignored each other in two of the booths.

The air smelled of cigarette smoke, and the floor was filthy with tracked-in snow. Keith took a seat at the end of the counter. An overweight waitress with dyed blond hair placed her cigarette on the lip of an ashtray, pushed herself into motion, and came toward him.

When she had covered half the distance between them, the indifference of her regard sharpened into curiosity. By the time Keith could smell the smoke on her clothes and her hair, the expression on her face said that her curiosity had passed into confusion, and she resented it.

"Why, you're just a kid," she said. "I coulda sworn . . . Anybody ever tell you that your face sometimes gives a person the wrong impression?"

"No," he said, which was at least technically the truth.

"No offense. I just thought you were older."

"You got any cherry pie?"

"Oh, all business now, are we? Yes, sir, I believe we still have one fine piece of our cherry pie left in the kitchen. Would that be your pleasure for tonight, sir?"

He didn't get why the waitress was acting all huffy and sarcastic. What had he done to her?

"Yeah, that would be my pleasure," he said.

"And what would you like to drink, young sir?"

"Gimme a coffee."

She frowned. "Are you old enough to drink coffee? Might stunt your growth."

He was going to tell her it was cigarettes, not coffee, that was supposed to stunt your growth, but it was too much trouble, and the world was seedy and poisoned all about him, just look at those mopes in the booths, dead already though they still drew breath. Keith slumped on the stool and said, "Okay, gimme a Coke."

"Sure, honey," she said, which surprised him. Then she gave him a greater surprise by bending over the counter and saying, "It can't be that bad, you know. Whatever it is. You're blowing it all out of proportion. I know, I really do."

"What are you talking about?"

"Whatever made you look so worried the minute you came in here. Honey, it put years on your face. You want to talk about it with me?"

"I'm not worried about anything," he said. "You're wrong."

She backed away. "Just trying to see if I could help you in any way I could."

"Help somebody else," Keith said, too loudly. It seemed to him that everyone in the diner had turned to stare at him, the old fart in the cap, the stiffs in the booths, the other waitress, the cashier, even the cook.

"One cherry pie, one Coke, comin' up," she said, and scribbled on her pad. By the time she slapped his order slip on the service counter, she was already taking a long drag, shaking her head, and blowing smoke all over the cash register.

The cook moved out of view, but the others, stiff as wax figures, were still looking at him with flat, two-dimensional eyes.

Keith Hayward bent his head and stared at the smeary patterns left on the counter by a wet rag.

In minutes, the waitress slid his slice of cherry pie and his soft drink toward him and vanished sideways without a word. He could feel the curvature of his spine and wondered if his new knife made a tent under his coat. He didn't care if it did. On the whole, he would be happier if the dreary people in the diner knew he was carrying a weapon.

When he bit into his cherry pie, he remembered to look at his watch. He wanted to give Uncle Till the full hour. That was his present, all sixty minutes, every one of its three thousand, six hundred seconds. That was a lot of seconds, and in each one of them, something only barely imaginable was happening. Though his pie was juicy, it tasted like dust. He could barely force himself to swallow the pulp in his mouth. When he tried to wash the cud down with Coca-Cola, the liquid in his glass felt oily and dead. It had no taste at all. The seconds had only barely begun to tick. Somewhere, a boy screamed and a man smiled. Inside his head, the screaming sank and flared like a candle flame on a terrace at night.

Maybe there was no screaming. Miller was not a screamer. He absorbed the pain and kept on going. Maybe he talked like an English teacher, but Miller, it turned out, was a goddamned soldier. For a second, Keith had a vision of Miller playing among the skulls and pelts, talking to himself, doing the voices of the dead animals. He had been like a child at those moments, and Keith had been surprised by the pleasure he took in this spectacle.

Out loud, he said, "I have feelings, too." The sound of his voice startled him.

The waitress, who had been talking with the cook through the service hatch, said, "Of course you do, honey."

Keith's head snapped back into position, bent to within only a few inches from his food.

"How's that pie working out for you?"

"I can't really taste it," Keith said. "I can't taste anything right now."

She planted her hands on her hips and came toward him. He heard her feet scuffing the floor, and the reek of tobacco smoke intensified.

"Would you like me to call someone for you, son?"

"What? No. I have to sit here an hour. A little less now." He forced himself to pull down his sleeve and examine his watch.

She leaned on the counter directly in front of him, but he did not lift his head. "Somebody told you to wait here for an hour?"

"I *gave* somebody an hour. The hour was my present. That's why I'm here."

Keith slid a small crescent of pie, less than a bite, into his mouth. It tasted like a dead animal.

She tried again. "An hour's a funny present."

"Maybe to you," he said around the bit of pie.

"But I suppose we could all use more time."

Without looking up, he swallowed the raw, oozing meat he had been chewing. The waitress watched him section off another tiny sliver of pie and slip it into his mouth. "Well," she said, "I'll let you wait out your hour in peace and quiet."

He nodded. The waitress scuffed her way back to the wall between the serving hatch and the cash register. The fat man in the greasy cap turned a page of *Life* magazine with the crack of a brisk wind snapping out a canvas sail.

Sometimes the pie in his mouth had the texture of raw flesh, at others it felt like cardboard. At intervals he glanced at his watch, always with dismay at how little time had passed. One of the silent couples left the diner, and ten minutes later a man rolled in on a tide of cold air, dropped onto a stool fifteen feet from Keith's, and announced to the waitress that he was fed up with Milwaukee and was looking forward to living in Madison, where he had just landed a good job at a mental hospital.

"J-job's a p-piece of cake," he said. "You j-just hang around this Common Room, m-make sure the d-ding-d-dongs d-don't fall down and swallow their t-tongues."

Keith tilted his head and peeked down the counter. The man who had taken the job in the hospital was about thirty, with a high, tight crew cut riding above his squashed-in profile. He was instantly identifiable as a bully, a grown-up Rocky Glinka. Keith snapped his head forward and gazed down at the little that remained on his plate.

"I'm strong, see? They l-like that. If the l-loony t-tunes act up, we p-put 'em in restraints. Or p-punch 'em out. You gotta be s-strong, or at Lamont?, they wouldn't look at you t-twice."

The Lamont Hospital sounded like every school Keith had ever attended.

"You're g-gonna miss me, ain't you, Avis?"

"We'll all miss you, Antonio." Her tone of voice,

at once muffled and sharp, made it clear, at least to Keith, that everybody in the diner detested the man.

"Now, d-don't you go feelin' s-sorry for me up there," said Antonio. "What's M-Madison, huh? Tell me. What's M-Madison?"

"State capital."

"That d-doesn't count. Come on. Come *onnn.* What else is it? That kid down there, he knows. Hey, kid! You! Kid!"

With dread and horror, Keith realized that the kid in question was himself. He raised his head perhaps a quarter-inch and risked a narrow glance at the horrid person now addressing him.

"Come on. Kid, t-tell her. What's the b-big thing about Madison, what's the b-big attraction they got up there?"

A single possibility appeared in Keith's mind. "The college?"

"The university, that's right! The big U! And what makes a b-big university like that so g-great?" He extended his arm and made an encouraging, keep-'em-coming gesture with his cupped hand.

"Umm," Keith said.

"You can say it, go on." He paused, and when Keith said nothing, generously answered his own question. "Girls! Girls from all over the s-state, from a-all over the country, thousands of 'em. *Thousands!* G-girls up and d-down both sides of every street, girls in every building, girls walking along those campus paths… hell, kid, I *know* you wanna go there and meet college chicks, right?"

"Uh huh," said Keith, who until this moment had never considered the possibility that he might go to college. It had not occurred to him that girls, thousands of them, might line both sides of a college town's every street. It certainly sounded more interesting than high school.

"Damn right you d-do. And you know what else? Soon as you c-can, get your ass into a f-fraternity. F-fraternity boys, they get hot and c-cold running dames."

"Sounds pretty good," Keith said, realizing that this was the closest thing to a normal conversation he'd had with anyone, including Miller, in months.

Evidently concluding that the boy had served his purpose, Antonio returned his attention once again to Avis. He wanted a burger, and he wanted it big, cooked all the way through but still with plenty of that good grease, and he wanted his fries so crisp you could snap 'em like twigs. And on toppa that. . . .

Keith stopped listening. He desired no more conversation. The one he'd just had called for certain internal adjustments, at present obscure in nature. Experimentally, he inserted into his mouth a section of cherry pie no larger than a dime and found on his tongue the chemical, metallic flavor of cherries long dormant in a can and congealed into a thick paste. For the rest of the hour Keith divided the remainder of the pie into ever-smaller sections, separated the pulp from the crust, which still had the taste and texture of cardboard, sucked the red mash off his fork, and wished it tasted more like actual cherries. Whenever he thought of Miller, he pushed cherrygoop around his plate until it melted into red gruel.

The check erased most of the dollar bill folded into his pocket. After he got off his stool and shoved his arms down the sleeves of his coat, Keith remembered Uncle Till's mention of tossing a five-dollar tip onto a bar and pushed a dime toward the waitress.

She smiled, and Antonio, his mouth full of well-done burger, nodded farewell.

The walk back through the cold and darkness seemed to take twice as long as he knew it should: chunks of time fell into a black abyss, and Keith came back to himself to find that he had gone no further than where he had been before he lost consciousness. He was taking the same step at the same place on the sidewalk, and he knew there had been a period when his body had walked on without him. Yet he had advanced not an inch, how could that be? The anomaly grew worse when he reached the appliance store with the long picture window. Between every other step, time vanished, suspending him in a void where he both moved and, apparently, did not. Minutes passed while he toiled past a hulking Maytag washer that through its huge circular eye mocked him for his inability to move beyond its reach. Silly boy, always dropping away, always remaining in the same place.

Silly boy, who . . .

Keith wrenched himself out of the Maytag's sphere and heard the hateful sentence die away and become nothing. This display of willpower kept him intact all the way to the narrow alleyway. He ducked in, and a wandering thought diverted him: *What kind of guy would actually like the idea of working in a mental hospital?*

Across the floor he went, guided by flashlight. He had left the door with the Medeco lock unlatched, and after he had opened it, Keith looked down the stairs to an empty, illuminated floor. To his relief, no sounds came from that realm. He realized something he had not previously understood, that he had been braced for screams, whimpers, quiet groans, the noises of Miller's distress. Down there, nothing seemed to be moving. Then he saw a shadow moving left-right across the gray concrete, and felt a quick, frigid blast of fear.

The shadow wore the shape of a human head. It occurred to him that on the whole he wished to hear at least some kind of noise from Miller. Absolute silence struck him as ominous.

"Uncle Till?" he called down.

"I thought I heard you," came Till's voice. "Enjoy your pie?"

"Sort of." He stepped onto the first tread.

"Did you order cherry?"

"Got the last slice." Keith came down onto the next step. "Wasn't all that great."

"You stayed there a long time, so I thought you were enjoying yourself. I certainly was. Best Christmas present I ever had. Weren't you, Miller?"

Miller neither assented nor demurred. Miller maintained a stoic silence.

"I guess he doesn't feel like talking. He's been working hard, old Miller." His uncle's voice came nearer as he spoke, and soon he emerged into view, wiping his hands on one of the old blankets. His jacket was off, and his shirtsleeves were rolled up just below his elbows. Beneath his hat brim, Uncle Tilly looked both weary and refreshed, and utterly at peace with himself. He smiled up at Keith. "Are you coming down, nephew? And what was wrong with your cherry pie?"

What was wrong was your Christmas present, he thought. "A guy told me I should go to college."

"Uh-huh. I see." Uncle Till nodded his head. "And that affected your appetite."

"I guess." Keith began to move down the stairs in the usual way, without pausing at each step.

"Sounds good to me, though. Get away from home for a while, spread your wings."

Keith took his eyes off his uncle and looked past him. Blood spots and spatters lay strewn like red lace across the concrete at the rear of the long basement. At the convergence of the delicate, brushlike spatters stood an empty wooden chair, its back and seat dripping with blood. Keith moved off the last step. His eyes followed a long, distinct smear of blood that ran from the side of the chair to a rucked-up blanket placed eight or nine feet away. A huddled white form covered half of the blanket, and that white form was Miller. Animal skins and torn posters hung on the wall beside him.

"Go check on your friend over there, will you?" Uncle Till stepped back and swept his arm toward the chair and the blanket. "I doubt he has much to say."

As he crossed the hard basement floor, Keith's legs felt like stilts. When he got to the blanket, he knelt beside poor Miller. Over much of his body, especially the arms, shoulders, back and legs, the whiteness of his skin had a blue tinge that spoke of the formation of deep bruises. Bright streaks and splashes of red covered his chest and obscured his face. Long straight gashes down the ribcage and inside of Miller's arms continued to leak blood. A big section of his hair had been ripped from his scalp, leaving a stippled pink-and-red bald patch that oozed red. Beneath eyebrows like thin dark pencil marks, his puffed-out eyes had swollen shut. Keith could see that a lot of the bones had been broken in the hands held cupped beneath his chin. His lips were purple. Tilly had also sliced into Miller's topmost cheek, and every breath opened a flap of skin, exposing his clenched teeth. His entire body was shivering.

Keith at last dared to bring the palm of his hand into contact with Miller's upper shoulder. The skin felt hot.

He whispered Miller's name.

"He's not going to say a lot, you know."

Keith jumped: he had not known that his uncle had come up behind him.

"It's up to you now, Keith."

The boy turned his head to take in his uncle's handsome, smiling face. "It's his time, son."

Keith blinked.

"Use your present on mine."

"Now?"

"He's half-gone already. Hell, the cold would get him if we just left him here. We can hardly take him to a hospital, can we?"

Keith looked back down at Miller's battered, shivering husk.

"Didn't you know that it was always going to turn out this way? Sure you did. You'll do me proud, kiddo. This is your graduation. Welcome to the world, son—I mean that."

"Tell me how," Keith said.

The phrase that had just trickled from his throat hung visible in the air before him, like frozen steam. He could not look at his uncle: he wanted to see nothing, nothing at all. The animals had turned their faces to the wall, happy to be dead and blind.

"I'll tell you everything you need to know, son," came his uncle's soft, caressing voice. "You'll do all the right things in all the right ways." A cold, cold hand patted his shoulder. "Reach around under your coat and fetch out that good-lookin' knife."

Keith groped around the small of his back, grasped the knife's handle, and brought it out into the light. It looked long, blunt, and businesslike.

"There you are, my boy, your instrument in your hand. Now scoot around a little higher on his body, so you're right behind the back of his head."

He managed a crablike shuffle that moved him about a foot up Miller's body.

The soft voice came again, folding itself toward his interior. "This part's real important, son, so get it right. Take your left hand and get it right around under that boy's chin. That's right. You're doing good now, Keith, real good. Pull that chin up away from his neck."

Keith raised the other boy's chin, awkwardly. The back of Miller's head dug into his thigh, and he inched backward to give himself more room to do what had to be done. He thought he could feel Miller's head turning feebly from side to side, but he could not be sure. Miller's whole defeated body was trembling.

"Now take your knife, Keith, and place it all around on the other side of his neck. No, farther, boy, farther. You want to do this right."

Keith settled the blade of the knife against the skin of Miller's thin neck, just beneath his chin.

"That's a sharp knife, so you don't have to do a lot of heavy pushing. Use your arm muscles and sink it in as deep as you can go. It'll just slice right in there, you'll see. Then give the knife a good hard pull all across the neck and jump backward, mighty sharp, because that blood's gonna leap out, and you want to get out of its way."

Keith braced himself to draw upon his muscles and sink the blade. Uncle Till tapped his shoulder and bent down to send even softer words into his ear.

"When this part's done, Keith, we're gonna burn down this building, and you're gonna retire from this business for a couple of years. I'll be gone—all my stuff is in the car. You go to college, you set yourself up in Madison, or wherever. You find another private room, and do your business there. You can do girls, but only one a year. Two at the most. Don't be in any goddamned hurry, son. Bide your time. Understand me?"

He nodded.

"Then go to it, Red Ryder."

Under Keith's grip, Miller twitched and uttered what might have been a word of protest that was instantly engulfed by the gout of blood that flew from his body. In the next instant, Hayward flexed his legs and propelled himself backward onto the concrete.

Till snatched the knife from his grip and swiped it against a blanket. He extended a hand to his nephew, who let himself be lifted to his feet. On the floor, Miller shuddered once, then sank into bodily quietude.

The next morning, Tillman Hayward had once again gone his mysterious way, and the *Sentinel* reported that a fire of unknown origins on Sherman Boulevard had destroyed an abandoned building and a neighboring appliance shop.

FRACTAL EVIL

——

Gary K. Wolfe

DAVID LETTERMAN USED TO DO A ROUTINE IN which he would display a news photograph and point to a minor figure in the background—sometimes goofy looking, sometimes vaguely ominous, sometimes nondescript—and ask, "What about *that* guy?" Straub is always asking the same question; hardly anyone walks into his world without a hidden story of their own, or several stories. If we want to know how the renegade Special Forces officer Franklin Bachelor in *The Throat* came to be such a soulless murderer, we can open a window into his childhood in "Bunny is Good Bread"; if we want to fill in still more about his later life, we'll have to wait for Straub's forthcoming graphic novel, co-authored with Michael Easton, titled *Tales from the Green Woman.* If we're curious about the reclusive and brilliant detective Tom Pasmore in *lost boy lost girl* or *The Throat*, we can find him as a child in *Mystery*, a novel published years earlier. Not every character is given such a backstory of course, and not every recurrent character is entirely consistent between different works—each novel and story has its own imperatives—but the implication is clear: what is toxic in Straub's world, like what is redemptive (though we don't get much promise of redemption in "A Special Place") extends beyond the borders of the tale. Such is the case with Keith Hayward and his redoubtable Uncle Till.

"A Special Place" occupies something of the same relationship to Peter Straub's novel *A Dark Matter* that the story "Bunny is Good Bread" does to his

1993 novel *The Throat*, so it seems particularly appropriate that Borderlands Press, which published that earlier tale (under the title "Fee" in *Borderlands 4*, 1994), should make this equally harrowing tale available to Straub's readers. Like that earlier story, it takes a seriously bad news character from the larger narrative and offers us a glimpse into key events of his childhood that helped shape the darkness within. And like "Bunny is Good Bread," it works perfectly well as a standalone story, leaving us with ominous portents of what this boy might become— portents that are partly, but not fully answered, in the larger novel. Keith Hayward may be an important figure in *A Dark Matter*, but it's not his story— and that, in turn, leads us toward a key characteristic of much of Straub's fiction, and one that lends a rich complexity to his body of work. Put simply, it is this: the closer we think we are to understanding the shape of the dark forces that often surround his characters, the more we learn that we've only glimpsed a portion of the whole picture. Like a fractal coastline that at first seems to be a clear border but upon closer inspection reveals a near-infinite complex of inlets, bays, and outcroppings, the nature of evil in Straub's world is forever receding from any definitive view: there's always another story, and behind that, yet another. Just as the Keith Hayward of *A Dark Matter* taunts us with the hint of an untold history—part of which we get here—so Uncle Till in "A Special Place" taunts us with intimations of his own untold horrors, and possibly the untold effects of these horrors on others, including his own family.

Embedded in the account of Keith Hayward's unholy tutelage is not only the story of Uncle Tillman's career as the Ladykiller—which may well involve murders beyond those reported in Milwaukee—but, at a more distant remove, the hinted-at stories of Tillman and Bill's older sister Margaret, or the gruff and cruel Detective Cooper. We're only given a single short paragraph about Margaret, who seems to have escaped the Hayward curse by marrying a millionaire in Minneapolis and changing her name to Margot, but for veteran Straub readers, she may carry a distant reflection of Tim Underhill's sister Nancy in *lost boy lost girl*, who also hoped that a normal marriage and family life could shield her from her family's past. If you read enough Straub, you can't come away from this paragraph without suspecting that something is waiting for Margot.

This complex of interconnected families and eruptions of past crimes is one of the distinctive marks of Straub's fiction, most thoroughly worked out in his "Blue Rose" series of novels and stories but implied in many other tales as well. His southern Wisconsin settings—"Millhaven," Milwaukee, Madison—begin to take on some of the psychic weight of Faulkner's Yoknapatawpha County, with the past never quite receding ("It's not even past," as Faulkner himself said), balances never quite restored, debts never fully paid. The horror in Straub's fiction doesn't derive from some overarching supernatural or alien agency (as in Lovecraft) or from one-of-a-kind monsters like Norman Bates or Hannibal Lecter (though Uncle Till could hold his own in this company), but from a kind of cumulative weight of bad karma: Uncle Till is frightening not only because of his blithe brutality, but because of the perverse familial pride he takes in educating his protégé, even to the point of recommending which

Hitchcock movies to watch (for attitude) and which knives to choose (for technique). If Detective Cooper were ever to succeed in tracking him down, it would at best be a partial victory, for the evil infection Till has set forth in the world continues to rage in Keith (and, as we'll see in *A Dark Matter*, Keith develops his own little band of followers).

The notion that crimes like Tillman's can never be fully eradicated suggests another important connection to Straub's fiction—that of *noir* movies and hardboiled writers like Raymond Chandler. It's almost a cliché to point out that these writers deliberately set out to provide a corrective to the classic detective story by portraying a complex and corrupt world in which the solution of a single murder fails to restore order to an otherwise innocent society (a point made at some length in Chandler's famous essay "The Simple Art of Murder"), but it's sometimes overlooked that a similar movement has taken place in horror or supernatural fiction. It's no longer possible to restore the world to normalcy by driving a stake through the heart of a single vampire, because there's never just one vampire anymore; a vampire isn't just a monster, but a *condition*. Much the same could be said of zombies and were-wolves—and for that matter, of serial killers, torturers, and sadists. In Straub's world, we rarely encounter the standard icons of horror fiction, but these human monsters are hardly even anomalies. In some sense, they're the pure products of America, the promise of the self-made man turned horribly awry. In a society defined by ambitions, Uncle Till offers one to Keith, just as Keith, on a smaller scale, offers one to the hapless Miller. In its own way, Till's suave manners and unusual proclivities, like Margaret's wealthy marriage, provides a path of escape from the lower-middle class drudgery of Bill Hayward's twelve years on the spray line at Continental Can. In Bill's view, "Tillman's good luck and handsome face had allowed him to escape the prison of blue-collar life. The man was a kind of magician, and whatever he did to remain afloat could not be judged by the usual systems." And indeed, the "usual systems" seldom succeed in restoring order to the chaos introduced by figures like Till; the mysteries are less likely to result in solutions than in *accommodations*, cases are forever reopened and reinterpreted, and in the end there always remains the suggestion of a Mystery that transcends the simple untangling of individual crimes. This is, essentially, the dual nature of the title of Straub's 1990 novel *Mystery*, a title that hovers in the background of virtually all his novels and tales since.

This is not to suggest that we should read Straub as some sort of social-protest writer whose monsters are bred solely by injustice and oppression; after all, one of his more chilling figures, Dick Dart of *The Hellfire Club*, is a successful lawyer and heir to a prominent legal firm, and few of his other killers show much in the way of economic or political motives. But the literary genealogy of figures like Uncle Till might well include such debased antiheros of naturalism as Frank Norris's McTeague or Vandover, such demonic tricksters as Raymond Chandler's Terry Lenox or Patricia Highsmith's Ripley, and of course Uncle Charlie in Hitchcock's 1943 film *Shadow of a Doubt* (with its screenplay co-authored by another American literary icon, Thornton Wilder), which Uncle Till so enthusiastically recommends to Keith. Such characters are neither the hapless victims of demonic possession nor uncontrolled psychotics, but rather intelligent individuals who, for whatever distorted personal reasons, have chosen and planned their careers. They are, in another dark reflection of classic American values, competent. Uncle Till is competent not only in technique, but in planning: he knows the importance of restraint, of limiting murders to one or two a year, generally not in your home town, and of keeping them quite separate from your family life. He is good at what he does, and it has offered him a degree of freedom and self-determination denied to the likes of his brother Bill, and offered to his nephew Keith. He's a brilliant perversion of a classic American type, in other words. But he's also more than this. He is, in a sense, a world-changer.

The critic John Clute, in his 2006 book *The Darkening Garden: A Short Lexicon of Horror,* uses the term "revel" to describe "the moment when a horror tale ceases to describe the welling up of the repressed and the subversive within the restraining walls of 'civilization,' and begins to tell it as it is."

Clute's outline of the horror tale, which begins with an initial glimpse or "sighting," continues into plot complications called "thickening," and leads toward revel and aftermath, could readily be applied to "A Special Place," as Keith gradually becomes aware of his uncle's activities, enters into a period of tutelage, and finally offers Uncle Till the Christmas present which leads to the offstage revels (acted out while the reader watches Keith trying to enjoy a slice of cherry pie), followed by the story's brief, one-paragraph aftermath. By the end, we realize that Keith has entered a changed world. We're not at all sure what will happen to him, but it seems evident that he can no longer return to the world that he knew before Uncle Till. "The field of the world is reversed," as Clute says, viewing this as a key movement within the horror narrative.

In the novel *A Dark Matter,* we will find out what happens to Keith, but it's hardly necessary or relevant to the internal dynamics of "A Special Place." What might be relevant is this: anyone who has read much of Straub's fiction, particularly stories like "Bunny is Good Bread" which are related to larger narratives, is aware of the relentlessness he brings to his most disturbing scenarios, his refusal to pull the camera back when we would expect a decorous edit from most writers. This almost loving attention to detail has the same effect as a traumatic experience. We know more about horrific events as they're happening than we will ever be able to understand later, despite all attempts at collapsing events into a narrative. (There is a bit of pulling back when we sit with Keith in the diner as Uncle Till is doing his business, but we soon realize we're not let entirely off the hook.) Stories like this very effectively distill the darkness of Straub's vision, but offer only fleeting glimpses of the light which complements this darkness—a light which suggests there is perhaps a seed of exaltation in extremity, of what Straub, in interviews and essays (and occasionally in his novels) has termed transcendence. In a story like "A Special Place," the possibility of transcendence may seem little more than the silences between the notes, but in *A Dark Matter* as a whole it's a theme developed as fully and directly as I've seen in any of Straub's fiction. That may well sound like a promotional blurb for the longer novel, but—assuming that by now you've read "A Special Place"—it's also a reminder that here, as with most of Straub's fiction, we're not quite getting the whole story, and that the youthful Keith Hayward, when he grows a little older and becomes a player in other people's stories, can become the instrument of something quite amazing.

As I said, there's always another tale.